NEVER-MORE

THE FINAL MAXIMUM RIDE ADVENTURE
JAMES PATTERSON

LITTLE, BROWN AND COMPANY
New York   Boston

Many thanks to Gabrielle Charbonnet,
my coconspirator, who flies high and cracks wise

_____

Copyright © 2012 by James Patterson

All rights reserved. In accordance with the U.S. Copyright Act of 1976, the scanning, uploading, and electronic sharing of any part of this book without the permission of the publisher is unlawful piracy and theft of the author's intellectual property. If you would like to use material from the book (other than for review purposes), prior written permission must be obtained by contacting the publisher at permissions@hbgusa.com. Thank you for your support of the author's rights.

Little, Brown and Company

Hachette Book Group
237 Park Avenue, New York, NY 10017
Visit our website at www.lb-teens.com

Little, Brown and Company is a division of Hachette Book Group, Inc.
The Little, Brown name and logo are trademarks of Hachette Book Group, Inc.

The publisher is not responsible for websites (or their content) that are not owned by the publisher.

First Edition: August 2012

ISBN 978-0-316-10184-4 (hc) / ISBN 978-0-316-20107-0 (International)

Library of Congress Control Number: 2011941034

10 9 8 7 6 5 4 3 2 1

RRD-C

Printed in the United States of America

To the Reader

THE IDEA FOR the Maximum Ride series comes from earlier books of mine called *When the Wind Blows* and *The Lake House*, which also feature a character named Max who escapes from a quite despicable School. Most of the similarities end there. Max and the other kids in the Maximum Ride books are not the same Max and kids featured in those two books. Nor do Frannie and Kit play any part in the series. I hope you enjoy the ride anyway.

Prologue
AFTER

IT WAS NIGHT, and Angel was perched on the hot surface of the scorched rock cliff. Her wings were spread out behind her, her ravaged legs swinging into nothingness, her ears straining in the strange new silence.

It seemed wrong, this silence. Shouldn't there be the din of destruction thundering around her? The crash of buildings sinking into rubble? Inconsolable wails mourning all that was lost? That the world as they'd known it had gone so quietly, slipping into the ether like an old, beaten dog, was disconcerting, to say the least. Wasn't noise what the apocalypse was supposed to be about?

Where was the chaos?

But there had been chaos, Angel reminded herself. Before. There had been plenty of screaming, fire and brimstone, and panic. She had endured enough panic to last her a lifetime.

Angel hugged her knees to her chest and folded her dingy white wings around herself, cocoon-like. She traced her fingers along her scars and fought back the memories.

Despite the warnings from nature—the earthquakes, the floods—despite all the efforts of science—Angel winced,

3

remembering the scalpels and fluorescent lightbulbs and blindingly white sheets—despite everything, in the end, the earth had been savagely claimed back for nature.

And despite Max's missions and the flock's preparations over the years, they still hadn't been ready.

But then, who could ever really be ready for the end of the world?

You, *Angel whispered to herself.* You were ready.

Angel squinted into the darkness. She couldn't see anything from her night perch on the cliff, but even in the light of day, the horizon didn't look like anything familiar or natural. You didn't see what was there—you saw the spaces between.

Watching Max fall had felt like that. Angel had imagined her grief as a blackness stretching out before her, the crushing weight of Max's death a night without stars, without hope, without end. It had terrified her so much more than the idea of Armageddon.

The power inside her was the only thing that scared Angel now. That she had seen how it would happen. That she had known. That she hadn't told anyone.

Angel tilted her head back to feel the chill of wind rustling her blond curls, now stringy and dirty. She listened in the silence. No whitecoats probing her, taunting her. No voices at all.

It almost felt like she was completely and totally alone. Almost.

Angel thought of the flock. Flying, diving together in one strong V, with Max at its center. She thought of Max holding her hand, calling Angel her baby. She wasn't a baby anymore.

How many seven-year-olds had seen the world go up in flames?

Angel shut her eyes tight. She waited for the visions she had fought for so many years before coming to accept and even depend on them. But no future appeared before her.

For the first time in her young life, Angel had no idea what would happen next.

Book One

BEFORE

1

"IN WORLDVIEW THIS morning, whole villages in the Philippines have been demolished, and hundreds are missing as typhoons triggering massive mudslides continue to wreak havoc."

I sat at the kitchen counter, staring at the small TV. The news anchor peered out at me with grave accusation. Yep, felt like a Monday.

"On the home front, officials rush to quell pockets of unrest as a subversive new movement takes hold in the cities." The camera zoomed in on a glassy-eyed fanatic raving about an advanced society and how we must act now to preserve the purity of the planet. He carried a sign that read 99% IS THE FUTURE. I shivered involuntarily. The newscaster raised one perfectly groomed eyebrow and leaned forward. *"Just who—or what—is ninety-nine percent?"*

The newscaster's face, frozen in practiced concern, dissolved into static as fuzzy black lines hiccupped across the screen. I frowned and smashed a fist down on top of the set, which only resulted in setting off a series of loud, plaintive beeps. Not that it was a quiet morning to start with.

Behind me in the kitchen, the usual chaos was unraveling. Iggy was slinging waffles at Gazzy and Total, who were trying to catch them in their wide-open mouths, like baby birds. How perfect.

"I can't find the socks that match this skirt!" Nudge said, holding up some floaty, layer-y clothing situation. A waffle whapped her in the head, and with turbo-charged reflexes, she snatched it out of midair and hurled it back at Iggy as hard as she could. It exploded against his forehead. "Don't throw waffles at me!" she screeched. "I'm trying to get dressed!"

Gazzy shot a fist into the air, his face twisted into that maniacally guilty grin that only nine-year-old angelic-looking boys seem to be able to master. "Food fi—" he began happily, only to stop at the look in my eyes.

"Try it," I said with deadly calm. He sat down. "Quit throwing waffles!" I yelled, snatching the syrup bottle away from Iggy, who was aiming it at his open mouth. "Use plates! Use forks!"

"But I don't have thumbs!" Total said indignantly. "Just because I can talk doesn't mean I'm *human*," he complained. For a small, Scotty-like dog, he had a lot of presence.

"Neither are we. At least not completely." I unfolded my

wings partway. Yes, folks—*wings*. In case this is your first dip into the deep end of the ol' freak-of-nature pool, I'll just put it out there: We fly.

Total rolled his eyes. "Yes, Max, I am aware." He fluttered his own miniature pair of flappers. Unfortunately, his mate for life, Akila, didn't have wings, so the non-mutant Samoyed spent most of the year with her one-hundred-percent-human owner. She had a hard time keeping up with us.

I shrugged. "So use a dog bowl, then." His nose twitched in distaste.

"I can't find—" Nudge started again, but I held up my hand. She knew I couldn't answer complicated fashion questions. She whirled and stalked off to the bathroom to begin her twelve-step daily beauty regimen—involving many potions, lotions, and certain buffing techniques. The whole thing made my head hurt, and since Nudge was a naturally gorgeous twelve-year-old, I had no idea why she bothered.

Iggy, who can't even see the TV anyway due to that tiny hitch of being blind and all, expertly manipulated the complicated wire system inside the set with one hand while the other continued to stir waffle batter. When the image was crystal clear and the monotonous beeping had ceased, he cocked his head, listening to the talking head deliver the morning doom with unbeatable pep.

"A new report has stated that steadily increasing levels of pollution in China have caused the extinction of a record

*number of plants this year. And could the growing number of
meteor showers we're experiencing require the implementa-
tion of asteroid deflection strategies? Dr. Emily Elert has some
answers."*

"Lemme guess. The end of the world?" Iggy asked.

I smiled. "Yeah, same old, same old."

"Next on In the Know, *Sharon Shattuck uncovers the
truth behind the growing number of enhanced humans among
us. Created for the greater good, are these genetic anomalies
an advanced race or an unpredictable risk? Heroes of science
or botched experiments? And what do we have to fear? Stay
tuned to find out!"*

My mouth twisted in annoyance. I leaned over and
snapped off the TV. It was time to get going, anyway. Why
had I agreed to this again?

A lot had changed for us in the past year, but one thing
had remained constant, and that was my unyielding loath-
ing for a certain activity that all "normal" kids—those
with homes, parents, and a distinct lack of genetic
mutations—seemed to engage in.

"Okay, guys, are we ready for school?" I rubbed my
hands together, trying to at least give the impression of
being mildly enthusiastic.

I studied the faces before me. Nudge's: excited. Iggy's:
bored. Gazzy's: mischievous. Total's: furry.

Someone was missing. Someone whose stupid idea this
whole thing was in the first place.

"Where's—?"

"Present," a voice said from behind me.

I whirled around and found myself face-to-face with Dylan. Actually, I had to look up slightly, since he was almost six-one to my five-nine. He gave me a slow smile and I wondered, not for the first time, how anyone could manage to look so flawless in general, let alone at butt-crack-of-dawn o'clock in the morning.

"Oh, good, you're up," I said, inappropriate thoughts running around my head like squirrels on speed. "About time." I coughed. "Everyone else is ready. We were about to leave without you."

"Um, Max?" Dylan said, dipping a waffle into a bowl of syrup. I looked into his Caribbean Sea–colored eyes, trying to ignore the little thrill that went through my body when I thought of the time I woke up next to those bright blues.

"What?" I asked, a little too defensively.

"You're in your pajamas."

2

"WHY ARE WE walking?" Gazzy's voice was plaintive.

"We're walking because other kids walk to school," I said, *again*, as I'd said every morning that week. "It's part of the whole being-normal experience."

Next to me, Dylan smiled. "And I appreciate your sacrifice," he said.

I tried to ignore his movie-star looks, with approximately zero success. Every once in a while his arm brushed mine, and each time it was like a tiny electric shock. Maybe it was a new trait he was developing, like an electric eel. (Don't laugh—stranger things have happened. Like when we bird kids developed the ability to breathe underwater.)

"I'm glad we're going to school," Nudge said, as she had every morning that week. Was this normalcy—predictable patterns, the certainty of doing the same thing every day? Because if so, normalcy was about to make me freak out and start screaming.

"Me, too," said Dylan. "Only for me, it's the first time, of course."

Dylan's had a lot of firsts since he joined the flock, but school was something he actually *wanted* to try. He was kind of weirdly obsessed with learning—especially anything about science. (Which I, of course, thought was totally repulsive. *Science = Wackjob Whitecoats* in my sad and tragic life story.)

"If it's your first time in school, it might as well be a schmancy joint like Newton," Gazzy said, and Dylan smiled.

I had to admit, so far our school week hadn't been a complete suckfest. Would I rather be home, doing almost anything else? Yes. Of course. I'm not *nuts*. But when our mysterious billionaire BFF Nino Pierpont, who some might call our "benefactor," had offered to pay for Newton, here in mountain-licious Oregon, Dylan had made Bambi eyes at me and I had caved.

Beyond the regular guilt trips from Nudge about wanting to lead a "normal" life, I felt kind of... *responsible* for Dylan. There was so much he didn't know about surviving. He might've looked like the original teenager he was cloned from, and it was true he was a kick-butt fighter, but

15

I had to keep reminding myself that this version had been alive only about two years.

Plus, there was that whole issue of him supposedly being created especially for me. To be my "perfect other half."

No pressure or anything.

I thought maybe he liked me more than I liked him, but still—once someone has kissed you in the rain on top of the Arc de Triomphe in Paris at sunset, you're kind of toast.

Anyway, agreeing to go to school with him—just for a while—didn't seem like that much of a big deal for me. The ratio of my discomfort to his happiness was acceptable. And because he's, you know, *perfect*, he fit right in at school and was already super popular. Because I'm, you know, *me*, I wasn't exactly super popular. Or popular. Or even noticed that much. Which was the whole point, right? Normalcy.

"Thank you for doing this." Dylan's voice was quiet, meant just for me.

I looked up at him, feeling the inevitable flush warming my cheeks. "Let's see how long I can stomach it."

He grinned. He didn't seem to mind that I wasn't all girly-girl and didn't have the smoothest of social skills. True, I was trying to brush my hair more these days, but I was still predictably clueless about clothes and how regular girls acted. Dylan seemed to accept me for me.

But why was I even thinking about that? Sooner or

later, his crush on me would end, right? And we'd go back to being—there's that word again—*normal*.

And just like that, my thin facade of agreeableness shattered.

"You know, life's not about being *normal*," I snapped.

Dylan glanced at me, one eyebrow raised.

"It's about being *happy*. And right now, what would make me happy is *not walking!*" And just like that, I took off at a run, then threw myself into the air, snapping my wings out.

I stroked downward powerfully and pushed upward, the familiar rush of exhilaration at taking flight filling me. I knew the other five bird kids—no, four—would be close behind.

I kept forgetting we were only five. There'd always been six of us (plus Total), but my flock had changed a lot recently. First Dylan showed up, then Fang left—don't get me started about that—and then, not too long ago... something happened. And we were down to five.

But I'm not going to talk about that. I can't. Not yet.

"Tag!" I felt a rush of wind and Dylan's hand tapped my foot as he rose strongly above me, his fifteen-foot wings shining in the morning sun.

I blinked at him, breathing in deeply, and the trees shrank below me, along with all those painful memories.

"Come on, slowpoke. You're it!" Dylan said, surging ahead.

Laughing, I soared after him, feeling a dash of pride. I'd

been the one to teach him how to fly, even if he was a wicked-fast learner. The two of us rose and swooped and chased each other until we were a block away from school. At one point I looked over at him, still smiling wide, and something seemed to light up his eyes.

"Normal's overrated," he said.

3

FANG OPENED ONE alert eye to see the early-morning sky lightening on the desert horizon. The slow, even breathing around him told him his gang was still asleep, and Fang felt the familiar weight of anxiety closing in on him snugger than his sleeping bag. They had to get going. He could feel it—the new threat was developing exponentially with every minute.

Get up, his instincts hissed. *Go. Now.*

But Fang felt the warm body in the sleeping bag next to his stir slightly in her sleep and knew there was something else entirely that was making it difficult to breathe. It was this whole situation. It was *her.*

He studied her relaxed features: the familiar cheekbones; the strong arch of the brow, making her look surprised in sleep like she never would in daylight; the full mouth he knew so well, the mouth he wanted to kiss, but wouldn't, not now...She still looked so heart-stoppingly like Max that it made Fang wince.

Fang wriggled up out of the cocoon of his sleeping bag and leaned over her. He reached one tentative hand out and ran his fingers through her short hair. She sighed.

"Time to get up," he whispered into her ear. "We have to get going."

"Stay," the girl murmured dreamily, pulling him back down next to her. She nuzzled into his neck and stretched one smooth arm over him. Fang swallowed. Even through the sleeping bag he could feel the heat coming off her body, sense the outline of her shape. It felt so natural, so familiar.

He felt so guilty.

Fang had never imagined he'd be sleeping next to a different girl, ever, in his life. And here he was, with Maya, of all people —Max's *clone*. The cute, short pixie cut she'd gotten two days ago helped. *No ratty mane to get tangled when I'm flying*, she'd said. But Fang knew she needed it for other reasons, too. She wanted to look different. To distinguish herself from Max.

And she *was* different. She was tough, but she seemed less angry than Max did, more accepting of her Gen 54 status. She smiled more often, and more easily. It made him feel way disloyal, but in some ways, Maya was just easier to be around than Max was.

Very carefully, with Fanglike stealth, he eased out from

under Maya's arm, lifting it and placing it back on his sleeping bag without waking her. He needed to...not be lying there anymore. He wasn't comfortable with where his mind—or his heart—was taking him.

One glance showed Fang that the members of his small gang—Maya, Ratchet, Star, and Kate—were all still asleep. He poked at the sleeping bags and shook some shoulders but got little more in response than annoyed grunts and thick snores. These kids were definitely not the light sleepers the flock had been. Fang sighed. First, some fuel.

The previous night's fire had been banked, and now Fang stirred the embers and added more tinder. Five minutes later he had a nice blaze, and he opened his wings, letting them bask in the heat. On the horizon, the sun was just starting to spill its pink glaze over the mountaintops. He tried to swallow the sense of urgency building within him. They weren't actually being chased, he reminded himself. He was in charge.

Years on the run had taught Fang how to make almost anything edible, including desert rats, pigeons, cacti, dandelions, and stuff reclaimed from restaurant Dumpsters. But this morning he had better raw materials to work with. He set the collapsible grill over the fire and pulled out a lightweight bowl and the one small frying pan he had in his pack.

Max was...Max. She wasn't easy, she wasn't restful, she wasn't a little dollop of sunshine. But since when did he need a little dollop of sunshine? It wasn't exactly what a life on the run tended to create. Max was... his soul mate. Wasn't she? She knew him better than anyone.

He cracked some eggs open a little more forcefully than he needed to and started whisking them in the bowl. He and Max had been through so much together—losses, betrayals, joyous reunions. Life-threatening injuries, gunshots, broken bones. Christmases and birthdays and Max Appreciation Days and Angel's—

A pain almost physical made Fang pause as he chopped the supermarket ham. *Don't think about that*, he told himself.

Anyway. Max. She was so familiar to him. *So* familiar. Maybe even... too familiar?

No! He couldn't believe he was thinking that way. She still surprised him, after all. It was just that he hardly knew Maya. He couldn't predict what she would say or how she would say it. It was all really... new.

He'd thought leaving the flock would simplify things, make things easier. Instead his life was just more complicated, more confusing.

He blinked when Maya's arms came around his waist. Only years of pseudo-military training had kept him from jumping a foot in the air. How had she snuck up behind him?

"Mmm," Maya said sleepily, leaning her head against his back. "That smells like heaven. Where'd you learn to cook like that? You're amazing."

Fang swallowed again and shrugged. "Just picked it up."

Maya came to stand next to him, one arm still around

his waist. Her hair was just so . . . cute. He blinked again in surprise. When had he ever thought someone's hair was *cute*? Not since . . . never.

Frowning, he looked down at Maya, who met his frown with a slow smile. She reached up on her tiptoes as he stood, frozen, and kissed his cheek. Her lips were cool and soft.

"Thanks for . . . breakfast," she said, and Fang got the feeling that he was caught in an undertow. And he didn't know if he wanted to get out of it.

4

AS A RULE, I like to remain an international girl of mystery. I err on the side of caution, to put it mildly, and we used to go to extreme lengths to not let regular people see us fly. But we'd been outed ages ago, and now we bother with non-winged-person camouflage only when we absolutely have to.

All of which explains why we landed right on top of the school buses in the parking lot, then jumped to the ground, where we were greeted with much wide-eyed amazement and murmurs of surprise from kids who'd been milling around, waiting for the bell.

I gave my shirt a little tug and unzipped my ever-present windbreaker. I felt stares and started to get that zoo-exhibit feeling. I bristled and put my shoulders back—

I'm all too used to dealing with people's curiosity, fear, and even, I dare say, a little awe.

Then I realized they weren't staring at me.

"Dylan!" A girl separated from her clowder (look it up—you'll learn something) and practically knocked me down to get to him.

"That was—" she began.

"So awesome!" another girl interrupted.

Right about then I noticed that these girls were wearing short skirts and spaghetti-strap tank tops, and had long, shiny hair. Trendy flip-flops emphasized dainty toenails painted blue and green and pink. It would be shallow to mention what I was wearing, so I won't.

If I'd been with Fang, he would have stiffened and then slipped away into the shadows before they even realized what had happened.

But I was with Dylan.

"Hello, ladies," he said, and his smile *visibly* took their breath away. I had no idea eyelashes could flutter that fast. Or why they would.

"I haven't seen anything that cool since Andi's couch caught on fire at our last party," said one girl, expertly flipping her hair over one shoulder.

"It was totally an accident!" the girl I guessed was Andi said, giving the first girl a little shove. Dylan's smile widened, and I waited for the girls to bow down and chant *We are not worthy!*

Except they clearly thought they were *so* worthy. Completely secure in their worthiness.

The first girl tapped Dylan on the chest with one painted fingernail. I stuck my hands in my pockets and fell back to walk with the rest of the flock.

"You're eating with me at lunchtime!" possibly-Andi said, smiling up at Dylan.

"And me!" said the other girl.

"And us!" Three more girls crowded around him and I had a sudden mental image of a bunch of hyenas circling their prey.

"I'm gonna have to get some wings," I heard a guy mutter as they watched the girls move with Dylan toward the school.

"Retrofitted wings are a disaster!" I informed him wryly, remembering my sometimes-evil, now-deceased half brother Ari's horrible grafted-on pair. The guy's eyes widened, and I got too late that he didn't *actually* mean he was going to get himself *wings*. In my science-gone-wrong world, it was only too possible, and I'd seen enough botched experiments to prove it.

"Sloan!"

Nudge's excited greeting made me look over to where a boy was loping toward us. He had smooth brown skin and a million thin dreadlocks pulled back in a loose ponytail. He was male-model cute, and I could practically hear the squeal Nudge was repressing.

"Hey, girl," Sloan called back with an easy smile.

"How old is he?" I hissed under my breath. Sure, Nudge is five-six, but she's only twelve years old, and in way too much of a hurry to get older, IMHO.

"I don't know," Nudge said blithely, heading off to meet him. I gave him a once-over—he was wearing a varsity jersey, which meant he was in at least tenth grade, probably eleventh. So, like, fifteen? Sixteen? Crap. What was she doing?

A light touch grazed my arm and I snapped my head sideways to see Dylan turning his full wattage to me.

"Catch you later," he said, and his sea-colored eyes seemed to look right into my soul. Again I remembered kissing him on top of the Arc de Triomphe. And a couple other places. Now he was throwing himself into the group of girls like chum into shark-infested waters.

Well, they can have him, I thought, touching my arm where his fingers had left a warm trail.

I didn't want him.

Right?

5

"WE NEED TO hit the road," Fang said to his small gang. "San Francisco's next up."

Maya squeezed his leg and flashed a smile that instantly eased his anxiety. "Ready when you are," she said, her eyes meeting his.

"Go, go, go," Star complained with characteristic attitude. "We just got here. At least let me finish breakfast." She tied back her silky blond hair and proceeded to house her entire omelet in one enormous bite. It reminded Fang of Gazzy gnawing every bit of meat off the hind leg of a roasted rabbit, and contrasted so sharply with Star's spotless Catholic-schoolgirl image that he had to smirk.

"What?" Star challenged Holden Squibb, who was also openly staring from behind his huge glasses. "You know my heart's beating like five times as fast as yours. Speed needs fuel."

Holden was the youngest, most awkward member of the gang, and his main skill seemed to be annoying Star. Well, that and being an incredibly fast healer. Came in handy, since he'd been horribly bullied in school.

"What's in San Fran that's got your panties in a bunch, anyway?" Ratchet was eyeing Fang cautiously. Regardless of his extraordinarily perceptive senses, after living on the streets, he could always smell trouble.

"Yeah, what's up?" Kate brushed her glossy black hair back from her face and followed Ratchet's gaze, looking worried. For someone with the kind of superhuman strength Kate had, she tended to look worried way more often than Fang was comfortable with.

"I'll show you." Fang flipped open his laptop and the others crowded around. "I've been tracking world news reports. A new threat is developing faster than anything I've seen so far. Three days ago there were five mentions of it. Two days ago there were five thousand. Yesterday, a hundred thousand different sources were talking about this movement. And today my Web counter shows more than a million mentions."

"You going to tell us what it is, or what?" Holden asked, showering the keyboard with toast crumbs.

"They call themselves the Apocalypticas," Fang said, flipping through tabs until he found their home page. "More commonly known as the 99 Percenters. I've done some hunting, and I think one of their bases is around San Francisco."

"99 Percenters?" Star leaned closer to read. "Please. That sounds so lame. At least the Apocalypticas sounds kind of like a rock band."

"I wouldn't dismiss them so lightly." Fang leveled his gaze at Star, and then at the rest of the gang. "You all remember the Doomsday Group."

Solemn nods all around.

"This is, like, the next level," Fang said. "The Apocalypticas make the Doomsday Group look like a glee club. They call themselves that because they want to start where the Doomsday Group left off—they want to reduce the world's population by *ninety-nine percent*, to obliterate all non-enhanced people."

Enhanced people. Fang and the flock had always called them *mutant freaks*, like themselves. Now it was *enhanced people*.

"Man, that is so messed up." Ratchet shook his head, the aviator glasses he wore even in darkness reflecting the screen.

"I mean, we're safe, though, right?" Kate said uneasily. "We're enhanced. It's not us they're after. Maybe we should . . . I don't know . . . stay out of the line of fire this time. We don't *have* to seek them out. Let's not forget what happened in Paris."

Once again Fang felt a stab of pain so sharp that it

almost took his breath away. As if he could forget. He bristled, frowning at Kate.

"Aren't you the *vegan*?" he asked. "The one who's always talking about the plight of other creatures and how we have to work together to make a difference? So now that things are getting a bit heavy, you just want to walk away?"

"It's not that, it's just..." Kate trailed off, looking sheepish.

"It's just that it's none of our business and we have ourselves to worry about," Star continued for her. Kate and Star stuck together because they'd been the only two freaks in their private school, but it was Star who had the mouth on her.

"What exactly are you saying?" Fang's words were low, measured. "We're talking about the human apocalypse."

"Come on, Fang," Star said harshly. "Don't tell me you've never thought that the world might be better if everyone was a bit more *evolved*." Fang gaped at her, but Star took it a step further. "Just look at Maya. She's like the next generation of your old girlfriend, isn't she?"

"Ouch." Holden gave a low whistle.

Maya's eyes narrowed. "What's that supposed to mean?"

Star shrugged. "I'm just saying, looks like Fang went for the upgrade. Shouldn't the rest of the world? Anyway, like Kate said, it's not us they're after."

"Look, you're welcome to leave at any time," Fang said, his eyes dark and furious. "You wanted the protection of the group, and I gave you that. I totally understand if, now that you're safe, you just want to slink away like a coward and let everyone else take the fall. I couldn't live with myself, but that's just me."

"Can you all just stop for a sec?" Rachet said, pushing his oversized hoodie back and tilting his head to the side.

"I can take care of myself," Star snapped at Fang, ignoring Ratchet. "I didn't realize being a part of 'Fang's gang' meant following you like lemmings over a cliff."

"Fang, Star doesn't mean that," Kate said, trying to defuse the situation. "You know we believe in stopping these maniacs as much as you do. We're just...we're nervous after Paris. We're still not used to being targets and all."

"Yeah, it must be really tough, being away from the cushy comforts of your private-school McMansions," Maya said icily, and Kate's face fell.

"Don't even—" Star started.

"You guys, *shut up*!" Ratchet yelled. He took in a deep, slow breath, his hypersensitive ears listening intently. "Something's coming this way."

Immediately Fang went on alert, jumping to his feet, putting the argument—as screwed up as it was—behind him for now. "Stow the gear in the van," he directed. "Maya and I will scout it out from above."

He glanced at the sky, cursing. It was maybe seven AM. They should have been on the road an hour ago.

"You guys, we're in the middle of the desert," Kate said. "Maybe we shouldn't freak out yet. There are tons of wild animals around here—coyotes and big lizards and turkey buzzards—and that might be what Ratchet's hearing. I really think we should keep talking this out, try to find some middle ground, and—"

Ratchet shook his head. "Yo. I can tell the difference between a fox or a lizard and...this thing. This mofo is big—bigger than a wolf, or even a bear. And I smell *blood*. Lots of it."

6

"I SMELL *BLOOOOD*," Star intoned in a deep voice an hour later. "Lots of it."

Ratchet scowled. "Say it again, girl, and see what happens to you. Go on—say it one more time. I'm telling you, something was out there."

"At least it wasn't worse," Kate said, her easy smile returning.

Fang nodded, glancing quickly in the rearview mirror. All he and Maya had found was a bunch of buzzards having a prairie-dog party.

"Yeah," said Star solemnly, "it could've been a small lizard, bent on destroying us all. Or a mutant desert bat, prone to feasting on the hearts of 'enhanced humans'. Right, Ratch?"

Holden and Kate couldn't help giggling, and Fang was

reminded of the flock. How many times had they joked with one another just like this, teasing and arguing? And here he was with a whole new gang. But the teasing felt harsher, the arguments more real. No flock in sight.

No flock, but there was Maya, next to him. She sighed unconsciously, like she felt as separate from the group as he did. It made sense. As the only two flyers, they could've made it to San Francisco in about forty-five minutes, but instead they had six hours of driving ahead of them.

Maya leaned her head on his shoulder. The bench seat in the front of their "borrowed" van meant she could sit really close, and she was.

Really close.

He breathed her in, ignoring the squabbling in the backseat, and an understanding seemed to pass between them. It was more than just having wings that separated them from the gang. They felt weird with the others because they felt *good* alone. Together.

Like he had with Max.

Just as Fang's thoughts started to spiral, Maya straightened up and frowned, leaning forward. "Do you see that? Like a dust cloud, way ahead, on the road?"

Fang squinted and saw what she was talking about: a growing haze, blocking the road ahead of them. "Ratchet?"

Ratchet looked smug. "I thought you guys didn't trust my senses."

Fang sighed. After the theatrics with Star and Kate, his gang was exhausting him. "Please?"

Ratchet sighed and lowered his sunglasses, peering through the windshield. When he spoke his voice was gruff, all business. "We got company. Looks like a convoy of vehicles, hogging both lanes and about to pay us a visit."

In seconds Fang had slammed on the brakes and made a tight, fast U-turn that sent the van up on two wheels. He stomped on the gas and shot them down the road in the direction they'd just come from.

"Sorry, but I'm not into sticking around for the welcoming committee," Fang said tersely, scanning the road ahead for the turnoff he'd seen a while back.

There was a slim chance that he was overreacting, that these were trucks taking vegetables somewhere or something. Fang estimated the chance of that to be approximately point-zero-one percent.

He accelerated more. He could feel the engine straining—and the van definitely wasn't up to off-roading. Fang watched the dust cloud advancing in the rearview mirror and felt Maya's tension next to him, her wings brushing his. It was tempting to break loose and fly...but no. They couldn't leave the others.

Fang breathed a sigh of relief as he saw the thin outline of the gravel road ahead. After the turnoff, they could ditch the van, flee to forest cover, and take whoever it was hand to hand. If necessary.

"Almost there," Fang muttered under his breath.

Half a mile...a few more seconds...

Wham!

7

THE IMPACT ROCKED the van sideways, and there was a deafening screech as it skidded across the asphalt. The doors on the left side were crunched shut. Windows shattered, Kate shrieked, and Ratchet started swearing—they'd been T-boned by a truck shooting out from the dirt road that Fang had planned to turn down.

Fang looked to his right and felt a tightening in his chest as he saw the gash, the slack jaw, the unfocused eyes. "Maya?" Fang said sharply, shaking her arm.

"I'm fine." Maya blinked, touching the blood at her temple. She smiled. "Just a bump."

Fang gave a brief nod and started climbing out through the broken windshield, reaching behind him for Maya's hand. Why was he worried? Maya could take care of herself.

"Out and scatter!" he ordered, and the gang started to scramble out the right side of the van. Fang leaped to the roof and did a 360. Two monster trucks blocked the dirt road, and four others had screamed into place in front of the van. The other convoy was maybe a quarter of a mile away and speeding toward them.

They were boxed in.

He surveyed the gang. Ratchet was holding a tire iron, and Holden had already assumed a battle stance. Star's speed and Kate's strength made them a fierce pair. And Maya...he had complete confidence in Maya. He'd seen her fight before, and knew what she was capable of.

In seconds, the other convoy was screeching to a halt behind the van.

Here we go, Fang thought, and felt his muscles tighten in readiness for whatever craziness was about to explode in the next thirty seconds.

For several moments, it was dead silent.

"What is this?" Fang heard Ratchet mutter. "I want to bust some heads."

Then, slowly, a door on one of the trucks opened. Fang tensed, ready to dodge bullets. But what emerged from the truck was a much more effective weapon, one that left Fang speechless, with his eyes bugging out of his head.

"Hello, Fang," said Ari.

Ari, Max's usually evil half brother, who was enhanced,

like the rest of the Erasers, with wolf DNA. Ari, who Fang had seen die, *twice*. He'd helped bury him! But... here Ari was. With a missile launcher balanced on one hulking shoulder. Pointed at Fang.

"Ari," Fang managed to say.

"I heard you were going to be the first to die," Ari said, his amused tone in sharp contrast to the crazy, feral gleam in his eyes. Fang shifted, remembering Angel's creepy doomsday prediction. "I wanted to make sure I got to do the honors." Ari pointed the heavy launcher on his huge, unnaturally muscled body at Fang. He smiled, baring long yellow teeth. "How about it, sport? You ready to die?" He tilted his head and looked through the gunsight.

For maybe the first time in his life, Fang felt... absolutely frozen.

8

"GUYS! OVER HERE!"

Dylan waved to me, Gazzy, Iggy, and Nudge from where he sat sandwiched between Eager Girl #1 and Eager Girl #2 at the popular-crowd lunch table.

I'd been headed toward the dweeb and misfit section, but when Dylan called out to us, Nudge squealed and hurried over. She confidently squeezed herself between some girls who looked less than thrilled at her arrival.

That decided it.

"Cover me," I said, sighing. "I'm going in."

"Got your back," said Iggy.

"Later, bye," Gazzy said, making a U-turn to go eat with some kids his own age.

I couldn't blame him. I, too, would rather eat with a

bunch of nine-year-olds than have to bear witness to the popular girls slavering over Dylan.

"Max!" Dylan beckoned. "Sarah, could you scoot over a little, please?"

Sarah looked like she would rather eat a slug than make room for me, but then Dylan turned his Pied Piper smile on her and she melted. She even patted the bench next to her.

It was almost scary, the effect he had. Thank God I was completely immune to it.

I sat down and a sudden silence fell as the girls looked at my heavily laden lunch tray. Dylan seemed oblivious, and kept up his easy conversation with Nudge.

"You must be...hungry," said one girl, whose name I think was Bethany.

I wasn't about to go into bird-kid caloric requirements, so I just smiled and said, "I don't have to watch my weight, thank goodness." *So bite me.*

Nudge popped open her juice. "Last night on *Project Makeover*, did you guys see where Tabitha was wearing those capris that looked like fruit salad?" she asked, her eyes wide.

Eyes quickly turned to her and heads nodded.

"Those were the ugliest pants I've ever seen," Sarah said solemnly.

I busied myself with my huge chunk of cafeteria meat loaf. Of that last exchange, I had understood the words "pants" and "fruit," but I couldn't see how they would go together. Then it hit me: Nudge really did fit into this world. I mean, okay, she'd told me that a thousand times. But seeing her like this, chatting with these other girls, normal girls—the only thing that didn't fit here was...her wings.

"How's your morning going?" Dylan asked me, ignoring the pop-culture bonanza surrounding us.

I swallowed, savoring the availability of lots o' food. To those of you who may sneer at cafeteria fare, I say: Try Dumpster-diving for a month, and then let's see how happy you are with Monday Meatball Medley or whatever.

"I'm at *school*," I said pointedly, and got that smile again, the one that seemed to suck the air out of my lungs. "*You* seem to be doing well, though." I slanted my eyes at the girls and then looked back at him.

He grinned. "Same old, same old."

"Uh-huh. Being God's gift to girls everywhere is just your cross to bear."

Dylan nudged my knee with his. "You think I'm God's gift?" He sounded horribly pleased, and I wanted to smack myself.

"No, but at least *you* do." I smiled and took a sip of juice. Dylan smiled wider and I felt a tiny thrill run down my spine. I knew I was courting danger, but this kind of easy almost flirtation was rapidly becoming addictive.

"I couldn't believe it when Terry said that orange was the new black," Nudge chattered on next to me.

"I know!" said maybe-Melinda. "I mean, *black* is the new black, you know?"

Nudge stabbed the air with a french fry. "Exactly! *Nothing* needs to be the new black, because black will always, *always* be the new black!"

There was fervent agreement around the table. I had no idea what they were talking about. Black *what*?

"Actually, it seems to me that *blind* is the new black," Iggy said, apparently deciding to shake things up.

"What?" a girl named Madison said.

"I mean, I can't believe there are so many blind students! A whole school of them!"

Silence. Nudge pressed her lips together; it had been going so well.

I started working intently on my square of spice cake.

"Um..." said Bethany.

"I know why *I'm* blind. Let's hear *your* stories!" Iggy waved his hand, "accidentally" flinging peas all over the people sitting closest to him. Nudge's cheeks flushed, and she stared at me, like, *Stop him.*

Oh, yeah, that could happen. No prob.

He turned to Madison. "What about you? Were you born this way, or did something happen to you?"

The people around the table looked at one another in uncomfortable silence.

"I'm not blind," said Madison.

Iggy pretended to look confused, then shook his head,

the soul of compassionate understanding. "You've got to face up to it. You can't let it hold you back," he said gently. "Denial is not just a river in Egypt."

"I'm really not blind," Madison said, looking confused.

Nudge gritted her teeth and stared down at her food, mortified.

Yep, we spread joy and sunshine wherever we go.

9

I TICKED OFF bird kids on my fingers. "Gazzy has Science Club today. If he blows something up, I will personally take a belt to him. Nudge is walking home, unwilling to be seen with any of us. And Iggy has soccer."

"I saw him on the field yesterday," said Dylan. "He looked great."

"He's always been good at it," I said. Somehow, Iggy's blindness had forced all of his other senses to overcompensate. His navigational skills and coordination were sometimes even superior to the rest of the flock's. "So can we fly home, or do we have to be normal some more?"

"Oh, I have something better planned, sugar drop," Dylan said with a twinkle in his eye as he led me to the school's parking lot.

"Call me that again and I will flay you alive," I promised, but I followed him to a large red motorcycle. "What's this?"

"I'm borrowing it," Dylan said, swinging one leg over the saddle. He patted the seat behind him. "Hop on."

I had been raised unburdened by the concept of "other people's property," so I hopped on. Dylan kicked the motorcycle into gear, and off we went.

I don't know if you have ever been on a motorcycle (if your parents don't know, please do not nod now), but I must say: If I didn't have wings, and if motorcycles weren't, essentially, extremely cool death traps, I would want to ride on one all the time. It's about the closest approximation to flying there is. The wind whipping through your hair, the sense of freedom, the bugs slamming into your face—it's flying, but on the ground, burning gasoline and making a lot of noise. What's not to love?

We didn't go straight home. I put my arms around Dylan's waist, leaned my head against his back, and closed my eyes. He felt warm and solid. I didn't have to do anything, *for once*—I just sat there. It was almost scary. Because I wasn't totally in control of the situation.

I felt the motorcycle slow, and then come to a rolling stop. Reluctantly, I opened my eyes. "Where are we?" I asked.

Dylan climbed off the motorcycle and held it steady while I got off. He waved his hand at the view. We were on the coastal highway, with rocky cliffs on one side and the Oregon coast in front of us. The ocean looked gray-blue and choppy, and the air temperature had dropped about fifteen degrees. Seagulls wheeled above the waves, cawing, and I wanted to join them.

I moved to the railing, ready to jump off.

"Wait, Max." Suddenly, Dylan's dazzling smile was nowhere in sight. His face was solemn, his eyes a darker shade of teal. For a second I thought he'd spotted some kind of trouble far in the distance, across the cliffs. You could say Dylan didn't just have the eyesight of a hawk—he had the eyes of the Hubble Space Telescope. His gift for seeing faraway things, especially in space, was a little mutant DNA bonus from the mad scientist-slash-genetic engineer who created him.

"I found this place the other day, when I was out flying," he said, shifting to a less guarded, more emotional tone. "I feel closer to the clouds here, more than anywhere else. I wanted to share it with you because...I feel closer to...to Angel here, too."

My eyes flew to his face, my mouth partly open in shock. Angel. The youngest member of our flock. My littlest bird.

I was assaulted with memories: Angel smiling sweetly at Total, her pale blond curls making a halo of fluff around her head. The depth in Angel's eyes when we witnessed disaster, way more knowing than any seven-year-old's should be. The way she'd get into my head, under my skin, inside my heart, always. And then—

Angel disappearing in a cloud of smoke. I grimaced, thinking of Paris and the explosion.

"We do not talk about that," I reminded him tightly.

He gave a sad smile and gestured out at the vast ocean, the craggy cliffs behind us. No one was around—it was me and Dylan, water and rock and sky. And my bleeding, ripped-open heart.

"You can't pretend she was never born," he said as I narrowed my eyes and pulled out my trusty standby: rage.

I opened my mouth to snap at him, but he continued, gently, saying, "You can't pretend she never died."

I actually gasped, drawing away from him in shock, feeling a sharp pain in my chest as if he'd plunged a dagger into me. *It'll be okay*, Angel had said the last time I saw her. *I'll be with you always*. But it wasn't okay. She wasn't with us. She never would be again.

"Shut up!" I croaked.

Dylan put his hand on my shoulder, holding me as I tried to spin away. He pulled me to him firmly, cradling me against his hard chest, one hand on the back of my neck, the other on my back. "We all miss her, Max," he whispered against my hair. "We'll always miss her."

And that was it. A horrible keening sound filled my ears, and it took me several seconds to realize it was coming from me. Then I was clutching Dylan's shirt, pressing my face against him, sobbing uncontrollably.

He held me tightly, his cheek against my hair, stroking my back and whispering, "I know. I know. Let it out, Max. There's no one here but me and you. Just let it all out."

I almost never cry. I keep my emotions on a supertight

leash. They normally don't just burst out of me like that, but once they did, I sobbed and sobbed until my throat was raw and Dylan's shirt was wet from my tears.

My baby was gone. After everything we had been through, after love and betrayal and fury and love and forgiveness, she was gone. Forever. She'd sacrificed herself to save thousands, and she would never, ever be back.

And I hadn't let myself believe that, until now.

10

I DREW IN shuddering breaths, my sobs subsiding. I had needed to grieve over Angel. And I had a lot of other things to grieve about, too. I'd been abandoned by my mother, my half sister, my pseudo-father, and the boy I thought was my soul mate.

And so finally, after all this time, I wailed my guts out. In a really loud, out-of-control, sloppy, wet way. All over Dylan.

I pulled away from him awkwardly. I was thirsty and empty and feeling hollow, and imagining the possible humiliation resulting from the revolting scene I had just made was vomit-inducing. "Remember that time you bawled like a baby?" Dylan would say for years to come. "That was hysterical!" I just wanted to collapse on my bed with the covers over my head. Forever.

But Dylan was still looking at my puffy face. "Remember how Angel saved that little kid from the hotel fire?" he asked, his eyes shining.

I did. I could still picture her smile shining victoriously out of her dirty face, the boy clutched in her arms, her wings gray with smoke. Angel, rising from the ashes.

I wiped my nose. "I'm done talking about her."

Dylan nodded. He was silent for a moment, looking out over the ocean. His hair looked dusty in the afternoon sun. "I don't know what to do with the sadness," he said finally, sighing. I looked up at him, surprised at his directness.

"Why do you keep talking about it, then?" I was too worn out to even get angry.

"I don't know what else to do." He shrugged. "I have all these hard feelings inside, and I thought talking about them might help. And...I don't want to forget Angel. I'm scared that if we don't talk about her, it will be like she never existed."

I nodded warily. I had my own hard feelings that I didn't know what to do with. They sat like a pile of rocks in my stomach. Building and building.

"You're the strongest person I know, Max," said Dylan.

"Yeah..." I picked at my nails, thinking about my meltdown. I had never been very good at receiving compliments, especially ones that seemed heartfelt.

"Seriously. I'm learning how to be strong just from watching you." Dylan put his hands on my shoulders. "But I know not everyone can be strong all the time. I just wanted to tell you that if you ever need to *not* be strong, you can lean on me. I can be strong enough for both of us—for a while, at least." He gave a slight grin.

Dylan looked into my eyes with such naked trust I had to look away. Below, the waves smashed into the rocks, spraying a cool mist over everything, and I felt goose bumps rise on my arms.

Fang always had my back—that is, until he didn't. He didn't have to say it aloud; I'd known it anyway. Dylan was so different. It was like he didn't know how to be guarded. His emotions were raw, on the surface for everyone to see, and the sarcastic wall that had protected me so efficiently in the past was slowly crumbling in the face of his honesty.

I felt vulnerable, exposed, so out of my element. I shifted uncomfortably.

"Can we fly now?" I asked, my throat dry.

Dylan smiled, his face lighting up, his eyes crinkling at the corners. He stuck the motorcycle's keys under its seat and took my hand, and we climbed up on the guardrail.

I took a deep breath, and together we jumped off.

11

THICK, HEAVY CLOUDS had rolled in, blocking the sun, and it felt like Dylan and I were the only two people on earth. Our wings took us high over the water, up and up until the cars on the highway looked like shiny beetles, bustling to and fro.

We wheeled freely through the air, no destination in mind, copying the gulls, seeing dark schools of fish in the water below. My chest expanded again, after being all crumpled up from crying. I felt my heart beating hard, felt the cool mist against my skin, and I felt fresh and alive and somehow lighter. Like I'd dropped some of those hard, heavy rocks I'd been carrying around.

Dylan was good for me, in some ways. I had to admit it.

"What?" he asked, raising his voice over the wind.

"What what?"

"You were sort of smiling."

I shook my head. "I don't know why."

"You know, Max," he said after a few more minutes. We'd slowly turned in a huge circle and begun to head toward home.

I looked at him, eyebrows raised.

"You know I love you."

I almost dropped right out of the sky. I literally forgot to flap my wings for a couple of seconds, and plummeted about fifteen feet before they started working on their own.

"I know you were *programmed* to love me," I said cautiously, rising back level with Dylan.

"Maybe I was," he said. "I don't know. I just know I do. And I know that love has to go both ways. You might not love me now, but I hope you will, in time. I can wait. I'm not going anywhere."

I said nothing, and we flew together wordlessly, higher and higher, as if we could touch the sky.

12

THERE WERE NO days. There were no nights. There were tubes and bright lights and indistinct voices. And pain. Always, always pain.

When Angel was finally put into a kennel, she whimpered with relief. This had to be better than the crisp white sheets, the stretcher that meant scalpels and masks and gloved hands always reaching for her. She shuddered violently, thinking of those hands, and shrank into herself. She never wanted to be touched again.

The kennel was meant for a large dog, but Angel still couldn't stand upright in it. She felt around in the cage, her hands brushing against the cool metal of the bars. She searched for a water bottle; her throat was sore from the feeding tube. She winced as she shifted her small body in the cramped space. She was covered with bruises, and her healing wounds stung.

Angel could hear muffled voices in the hallway, echoes of footfalls on the linoleum floor, the squeak of rolling wheels—seemingly innocuous sounds that now haunted her dreams—but she didn't cry out. She was way past that.

"Help!" she had shrieked at first, for days it seemed, as loud as she could. And later, when it was clear no help was coming, she had only croaked "Why?" as they probed and prodded, her voice a thin, wheezy rasp. But there were no answers, so she had stopped asking.

Angel had always felt stronger and more capable than everyone—well, than Max—thought she was. But in the end, she was still just a little kid, with bones that could snap and a heart that could break.

She was broken. And totally alone.

A long, silent sob trapped in her chest, Angel curled up on the thin towel in the corner of the kennel and went to sleep.

"Wake up!" a voice barked after what seemed only moments.

So it wasn't over, then.

Her heart raced in time to the familiar fear, the dread that made her whole body quiver, but Angel resisted. For several long, delicious moments she allowed herself to indulge the fantasy that it was Max calling her to wake. Even if they were on the run, even if Max was being bossy, even if... Well, anything would be better than the reality she would find when she opened her eyes.

"Wake up! There's no sense pretending! Your brain waves show you're awake."

Her blue eyes fluttered open just as a bucket of icy water was dumped on her head. Gasping, Angel scrambled farther into her corner, but she was a trapped animal, and she knew it.

The back of her head stung unbearably from the icy water and she tentatively touched it with her fingers. A small section of hair had been shaved, and a neat line of small stitches made tiny ridges under her fingers. They'd operated on her brain. A pitiful cry escaped her lips.

Max, Angel thought frantically, overwhelmed with horror. *Max—help!*

13

"LOOK HERE," the voice commanded. "Pay attention."

Angel blinked water out of her eyes and squeezed her hair, feeling chilly rivulets trickling down her back. Outside her crate, the room went dark. Angel saw extremely well in the dark, but then a lit screen flickered on, several feet away.

She saw a young child, a boy, with pale, almost white hair. He was lying on a table, very still, covered with a sheet. A crisp, white, sterile sheet. Angel shuddered involuntarily, the wounds on her body aching in response to the image.

The camera panned to look down on the boy, and Angel saw that he was in an operating room. He had a mask over his nose and mouth, and his eyes were clamped open.

Angel recognized the look in them. It was a feeling she knew well: pure, undiluted terror. Angel felt an icy coldness in her temples as the view zoomed in. There, on the little boy's neck, was the trio of freckles, right where she knew they'd be.

Iggy.

It was Iggy as a little kid. Before...

Angel swallowed hard, her eyes trained on the large screen as gowned and masked doctors came in and shone spotlights onto Iggy's operating table. One doctor, his eyes hidden behind large magnifying glasses, spoke directly to the camera.

"Today we're experimenting with a new technique, only recently developed. It involves a surgical stimulation of a certain area of the rods and cones in the backs of this hybrid's eyes. We estimate that the subject will have its night vision improved by at least four hundred percent."

Then Iggy's panicked blue eyes filled the screen.

Angel shook her head, horrified. She couldn't watch. They weren't really going to make her watch...?

But the video continued, and she couldn't look away. She stared as the scalpel found its mark and plunged in as if slicing a boiled egg, as tweezers pinched and needles probed, as blood pooled and tubes suctioned it away.

As they hacked into him, like butchers.

She listened as Iggy's agonized moans grew more and more frenzied. They sounded visceral, verging on madness, louder and louder and louder.

He was awake. The whole time.

Angel shrank back into her crate and squeezed her own eyes shut, the screams echoing in her ears. She had just seen a film of the crazy whitecoats at the School making Iggy blind.

"No!" she wailed, her voice joining Iggy's. *"No no no no."*

The movie flickered to a stop and the room's lights came back on.

"That was thirteen years ago," someone said from out of view. "The techniques were unbelievably primitive, which no doubt caused the less than optimum results."

Less than optimum? Angel thought with rising hysteria. *You mean the total blindness? That result?*

Once again she tried to hack into someone's brain, the brain of even one person in this awful torture chamber. But it was like the room itself had a dampening field—she hadn't been able to read a single thought the whole time she'd been there.

"But you see, Angel," the voice went on smoothly, "we've made tremendous progress since then. Those were the days of cavemen. The science, the technique, is vastly improved. This time, it will go beautifully."

"No," Angel whispered again, her adrenaline surging and making her voice seem small, fuzzy. "No, please—"

A gloved hand reached for the door of her crate.

This time, they would operate on Angel. On her eyes.

14

"ARI, WHAT ARE you talking about?" Fang said. "We're on the same side, remember? You saved Max."

"Times change." Ari smiled again and looked down the sight of his missile launcher, as if gauging how far away Fang was. Fang shifted his weight, primed to leap. "Having the same goal doesn't mean we're on the same side."

"What—" Fang began, but he was cut off by a chorus of deep growls. Four more thugs climbed out of the truck to stand behind Ari, looking like a row of college linebackers. Their resemblance to Ari was freakish, surreal: They had the same glint in their eyes, the same unnatural, stretched-out features, the same wolfish undertones. Clones? Or just well-made copies? Fang didn't want to stick around long enough to find out.

"Fang, who *are* they?" Star hissed. She was standing beside Kate, her face even tenser than usual, and Holden was right behind them. Ratchet was glowering at these ugly strangers, smacking the tire iron against his palm. Maya stood silently at Fang's left wing—Fang remembered that she knew Ari.

"Erasers," Fang answered quietly. "Human-wolf hybrids. Except they're supposed to be extinct." *So how was Ari alive?*

And more important: *Why was he suddenly evil again?*

Maya met Fang's eyes. *Fight or flight?*

"Enough talking," Ari said, almost lazily. "Let's play a game!"

Fight.

15

BEFORE FANG HAD time to think, Ari fired a missile.

Right at him.

Instantly, Fang unfroze, his instincts going from shock to hyperdrive in zero point two seconds. "Duck and cover!" he barely had time to shout as he threw himself sideways off the van. The missile missed Fang by a hair, singeing his shirt as it shot past.

And then—*boom!* Their van exploded in a mushroom of flames, flying metal, and roiling black smoke. Kate shrieked as a shard of glass swiped across her cheek, leaving a thin line of blood, but the sound was just barely audible above the roar of the fireball.

Fang jumped to his feet, ears ringing. The van was

nothing but a few smoldering, smoking chunks scattered in a circle around the blast zone.

Holden scrambled to his feet, dust-covered and wide-eyed, as Kate wiped blood from her cheek. Ratchet was hardly visible through the thick black smoke. "Man! Friggin' almost busted my ears!"

"Never really liked that van anyway," called Star, a little shakily. She, unlike the rest, looked perfectly unharmed and clean—the ability to be forty yards away in the blink of an eye sure did come in handy.

Fang's gang dropped into their battle positions, but they all looked a bit wigged out. Even Fang was tense with an apprehension he wasn't used to. Ari was a wild card, and even after all the training they'd done, even with their advanced abilities, he didn't trust any of the gang under pressure like he had the flock. Well, any of them except...

Fang could make out Maya's shape walking toward him through the dust cloud, her wings outstretched, looking powerful and ethereal in silhouette.

We'll be okay, Fang thought.

"Aw, I missed," Ari said in his rusty voice. He was still grinning wickedly, like a tiger cornering its prey. "Enough of the theatrics. Let's *do* this thing, Fang. You and me. Let's make some history here, before your freaky friends get hurt."

"Works for me," Fang snarled, but to his surprise, Maya's hand shot out in front of him. She stepped forward, putting herself between Ari and Fang.

"Hey," she said to Fang. "Sorry—I got thrown. But listen: If we fight, we fight together. We're a team. Got it?" Fang nodded, knowing there was no use arguing. She was as stubborn as a mule.

Like someone else he knew.

"Can't ever just stay out of it, can you, Max?" Ari shook his head. "You're looking a bit rough, sis. The hair's a little G.I. *Jane*, don't you think?"

"Not Max. *Maya*," she said, running her fingers through her short pixie cut.

Ari laughed, his yellow fangs glinting. "Oh, yeah, Max II. That explains it, then—the delayed reflexes, the bravado. The life of a clone, so difficult." Ari pouted in mock sympathy, and Maya's eyes narrowed. "We understand your pain, don't we, boys?" The row of Erasers behind him twitched impatiently, growling and muttering. "I have to say, though, Deux—as clones go, you seem like more of a cheap imitation. Did Fang pick you up in the discount aisle?"

"I said, the name is *Maya*," she repeated, jaw clenched.

"Same, same," Ari said, still smiling. "Fresh meat either way."

And then, before Fang could even react, all heck broke loose.

Maya crashed into Ari, her eyes furious and vengeful, knocking the missile launcher out of his grasp with one swift kick.

Fang lunged toward them, protesting. Team or no team, Ari was *his* fight. But in their adrenaline-boosted frenzy, Ari's goons leaped forward, driving Fang and the rest of the gang into defense mode, away from one another.

Away from Ari and Maya.

16

FANG WAS BACK in his comfort zone—that is, beating the living pus out of freaking Erasers, as usual.

I have to get back there, Fang thought, trying to see through the wall of hulking bodies. Maya was hard core, but Fang had known Ari to be a vicious fighter, and this new version of Ari would likely be even tougher.

After he finished off another Eraser, blood from the guy's nose spattering his black feathers, Fang pushed off the dusty ground and did an up-and-away. He hovered about fifty feet up, searching the scene.

There, near the demolished van, landing blow after blow, was Maya, holding her own. Ari was no longer smiling. He was clearly sweating with the effort, and his face was furious. And surprised. Fang almost smiled. Maya was fearless and graceful and merciless. She was beautiful to watch.

He scanned the road and spotted Holden backed into a corner with an Eraser. Fang frowned. The kid's technique was all off, and he looked terrified and in way over his head. The Eraser advanced on him, murder in his feral eyes.

The Eraser tore into Holden's arm and raised his claw for the final blow, and Fang dove.

The dive was short and lightning quick—the half-dazed Eraser never saw him coming.

Fang stood up, looking around for Holden, and caught a glimpse of Ratchet wailing on some guy with the tire iron...right as Kate paused in her own fight and clipped Ratchet under the chin with her left hand, sending him reeling backward.

"Kate!" Fang yelled sharply. "Watch your aim!"

Ratchet was already standing back up, looking annoyed but ready to take on the next Eraser, when Star, appearing out of nowhere, spun him around just in time for Kate to land another bone-crunching blow to his chest. As Ratchet crumpled to the ground, the Eraser gave Kate a brief nod of acknowledgment.

Fang's insides turned to ice as things clicked into place: how the convoy had found them, why the two girls had looked so freaked out. They hadn't been nervous about the fight.

They'd been nervous about their betrayal.

"Traitors," Fang hissed, advancing on them.

Kate shook her head slowly, apologetic. Guilty. "Sorry, Fang, we wanted to help you. It's just that..."

"Survival comes first," Star said simply.

Before Fang could respond, two Erasers charged toward him, and everything was a blur of color and instincts.

Fang, on autopilot, kicked and dodged, feeling hollow, anger driving him as he beat the freak out of the guys while Star and Kate just *watched*.

With a last surge of adrenaline he crushed the windpipe of the final Eraser, and then it was over.

Everything was eerily quiet without the sounds of battle.

"Starfish," Fang called to Holden. "You all right?"

"Yeah," the kid said, wincing as the cells in his arm multiplied, the deep gash closing before their eyes.

Fang nodded. His side felt bruised, he had a possible cracked wing bone, his arms ached, and a gash on his forehead dripped blood into his eyes. It had felt so satisfying, sweating through his fury. *Hurting* someone. But now that it was over, Fang still had to deal with *this*.

Betrayal.

17

FANG STOOD FACE-TO-FACE with Star and Kate, fists clenched, breathing hard. His muscles stood out on his arms. He felt his agitation vibrating to his fingertips.

Kate looked uneasy and shifted into a more defensive stance. She looked scared. Of him.

Star, on the other hand, looked unrepentant. She looked him straight on, her blue eyes cold and determined. If he was going to attack, she was ready.

Holden looked up at Fang, waiting for his cue. His eyes were wide with anticipation, but he remained loyal. He had Fang's back.

Was he going to attack? For one of the very few times in his life, Fang had no idea what to do. Should he scream, walk away, or finish them completely? The unasked question hung in the air between them, the tension building. Fang's face twitched. He was furious, but mostly he just felt disappointed.

Only one other situation made him this stressed, this confused...this freaking *emotional*. He looked around. Where was she?

Where was Maya?

And Ari?

"Fang!" Holden grabbed his sleeve. "Up there!" He pointed at the sky.

Fang looked up and felt his heart stop.

Maya and Ari. Five hundred feet up.

Battling to the death.

18

THEY HEARD HER scream pierce the air even from the ground, saw the bright arc of blood splash across the sky. And then she was falling.

Fang felt dazed as he watched her floating down, a long sigh stretching out between them, arms and legs reaching lazily upward, feather-light, body pulling down.

Go, Fang's instincts shrieked at him, but time had stopped. He was frozen to the spot, and so was she.

Suspended. A picture snapped, a painting hung against the endless wall of sky. *Still life of a tragedy*, Fang thought. He felt a bright wave of distress, his heart thundering out of his chest, but he couldn't connect the feeling to the image in front of him.

Her wings were silhouetted against the brilliant flame

of sunlight. Fang knew the exact color of those wings, their span, their texture against his cheek. Hawk's wings, to match her sharp instincts, her hard looks.

She looked soft now—softer than the air and the clouds around her. Tender. Cradled in blue.

Fang was holding his breath.

He could see her face now, her mouth open in a perfect *O*, caught in mid-sentence, drawing in.

To tell him everything that had never been said. That she'd still be there for him, like she always had. That he shouldn't have left her and the flock.

That she loved him.

Fang felt his will seeping out of him, crushed beneath the weight of this knowledge. The fall would kill them both.

He blinked and she was moving again, her arms like a marionette's, in unlikely poses, twisting. A delicate dance, a swaying to music he could not hear.

Down . . . and down.

Her features came sharply into focus and Fang saw the fear there, her mouth protesting in a silent scream, the ragged ripple of wing tearing behind her, ruined.

The blood in her hair, cut short. So it wouldn't get tangled in the wind.

The sound caught up to Fang's ears, the shriek vibrating louder and louder, closer and closer as the ground rushed upward and all the light fell away from her and she was plummeting, as dark and heavy as a stone.

Max—no, *Maya*—was falling to her death.

Fang surged upward. Racing gravity, he stretched out his arms toward Maya's free-falling body. He just barely managed to catch her, then sagged as her deadweight dragged him down.

Hovering with Maya clutched in his arms, Fang felt his jaw tighten as he saw that her neck was covered in blood, which was streaming down her skin and onto her shirt. *No, no, no*, his brain protested with growing distress. Ari's claws had sliced her up like deli meat.

"Fang," Maya whispered.

"You're okay," Fang said, as much to convince himself as Maya. "I've got you. You're okay."

Scenes flashed in Fang's mind: Maya laughing easily. Maya asking if he was okay, her eyes soft, concerned. Maya after her haircut—happy, confident, ready for a fresh start. He hadn't wanted to admit it, but he had thought they could be each other's fresh start. He ground his teeth into his lips to keep from screaming.

"Fang...I love you," Maya said, starting to cry. Tears trickled over her lovely cheeks, down her jaw, into the mutilated mess of her neck.

The sound of wings filtered into his brain, but only vaguely, as if he were hearing it through a long tunnel.

"I know," Fang whispered.

Then he felt the wind shift behind him, felt the hairs on his neck rising. Before he could move, before he could react, Ari appeared, and with a final, murderous lunge, smashed his elbow into Maya's chest with crushing force.

"No!" Fang screamed as Ari soared away from them. Still struggling to hold Maya up, Fang couldn't defend her, couldn't fight back. He could only clutch at her and watch it happen.

Helpless.

Fang landed as gently as he could. He fell to his knees, arranging Maya's head on his lap.

"Crap," Ratchet said, awake again and limping over. "I saw Ari take a swipe at her, but I didn't think it was *that* bad."

"Get me something to stop the bleeding," Fang said tersely. Ratchet looked around, then grabbed Holden and yanked the boy's shirt off. He tossed it to Fang, who pressed the cloth to Maya's neck.

He was aware of Star and Kate, unsure what to do, huddling together off to the side. They clearly hadn't been prepared for this. Fang would deal with them later.

Ratchet and Holden leaned silently over him. They knew, just as Fang knew, that it was too late.

"I'm sorry," Maya cried helplessly. She coughed and sputtered, her breath growing shallow.

"Shh," Fang said. "Don't talk. Just focus on breathing. You're going to get through this. *We're* going to get through this," he repeated.

Maya's brown eyes struggled to focus on his. "Sorry I'm ... not st-strong af ... ter all."

"Maya," he said quietly. "You *are* strong. Stronger than anyone."

"After Max," she said, trying to smile. Blood began to seep from beneath Holden's shirt and drip on the ground.

Fang shook his head. "Not after Max. Right next to her. Equal."

"Thank you," Maya whispered. Then her eyes seemed to focus on a spot just to one side of Fang's face, and her head lolled.

Fang didn't move.

He just sat there, staring at the dead girl. The dead Maya, the dead Max, the dead almost everything he cared about. He felt like a freight train was slamming into his chest, over and over again.

Ratchet and Holden tensed beside Fang as footsteps approached. Ratchet said, "Fang? Wolfboy's back."

Still Fang didn't move from his place on the ground, didn't stop cradling Maya's body.

Ari's voice, gruff and taunting, cut through the fog. "Fang—sorry, man. Had to happen. Don't worry, though— she's a clone, right? Dime a dozen."

Finally Fang looked up, his eyes swimming. "We'll finish this later," he said through clenched teeth.

Ari grinned. "I'm counting on it," he said, turning. "C'mon, you weaklings, get up," he shouted at the injured Erasers. Many large bodies heaved themselves noisily toward the trucks.

"Coward!" Ratchet hurled the dented, bloodied tire iron through the air.

Ari stepped swiftly to the left, and the metal clanged

against a truck. His laughter, grating and harsh, filled the empty desert battlefield. Then the engines roared and the entire convoy spun around and faded away in a cloud of dust.

When they were gone, Fang passed his fingers over Maya's face, closing her eyes and brushing away some blood. He forced himself to lay Maya's already cooling body on the ground. As Fang looked down at her, he wanted to tear his own heart out.

Ari would die for this.

19

AS SOON AS I walked into biology class, the nauseating smell of formaldehyde hit me smack in the face. *Hello, butt-load of horrible memories!* Clearly today was going to be even more nightmare-y than school usually was.

"Hello, Max. Glad you could join us," Dr. Williams said.

Frowning, I nodded and plopped down beside Dylan as jealous girls nearby prayed for my death. So I got side-tracked by the schmanciness of the bathrooms on the way here. Sue me.

The smelly chemicals were already getting to me (read: making me want to run away screaming), and I could tell they were also bothering Iggy, who was sitting a couple tables over. His face was drawn and even paler than usual.

Dr. Williams passed out packets of paper. "Today we'll be doing our first hands-on lab assignment," he said. "For some of you, this will be your first dissection. It's a very simple one, but if anyone feels sick, the trash can is right here. Please try to make it."

Dissection.

Oh, God.

I glanced down at my packet and my stomach dropped. *Chicken Dissection Lab.*

Of course. This was *my* life, after all—if something could conceivably get worse, then by golly, it would get worse. We couldn't just dissect a frog, or an earthworm, or whatever. We had to dissect something with *wings*.

The other students chattered around me, their reactions ranging from excited to grossed out. Iggy, Dylan, and I were the only silent ones.

Dr. Williams began handing out plastic bags containing rubbery chicken carcasses. I fought back a wave of panic and nausea as I skimmed my info packet. Phrases like *Count the number of primary feathers* and *Remove the heart* and *Examine the air sacs* popped out at me.

Please, if there's any justice at all in this screwed-up world, please *don't make me have a mental breakdown and start hyperventilating in front of my entire biology class.*

Dr. Williams placed a plastic bag on our table, two feet

from my nose. Dylan and I both stared at it, unwilling to touch it.

"Okay, folks," Dr. Williams said merrily. "Get your goggles, your gloves, and your trays. The packet explains everything, but come to me if you have questions. Happy dissecting!"

20 .

I PUT ON my clear, dorktastic goggles automatically while Dylan fetched the dissecting tray. It was equipped with a scalpel, a small pair of scissors, three pokey, suspicious-looking tools, and a pair of tweezers.

"So," I said, mentally smacking myself upside the head when my voice shook. "Ready to cut this thing open?"

"We can leave, if you want," Dylan replied softly. "I don't want to do this any more than you do."

I clenched my teeth and pulled my shoulders back, shaking my head. "No. Normal people do dissection labs. And we're normal people, remember?"

He nodded, his aquamarine eyes fixed on me.

I regretted my decision almost as soon as we set the chicken on the tray. It splayed out pathetically, headless and mostly featherless, with puckered pink skin. I felt the chill of goose bumps on my own flesh and shivered.

The chicken's wings were small and had tiny tufts of down still stuck to them.

White down.

Like Angel's.

"Step one," Dylan read aloud. His voice cracked and he cleared his throat. "Place chicken on its back. Grasp both legs and push down and away from the pelvis."

In another time, I might have snickered immaturely at the word "pelvis." But at that moment, all I could do was numbly follow the instructions, while trying to block smells and memories.

It was bred for this, I reminded myself, holding the scalpel. Inside a claustrophobic metal cage, it had been fed scraps. It had been genetically manipulated for a satisfactory amount of plumpness and complacency. It had been bred with a smaller brain, too; it was too stupid to see how trapped it was. To see that this is how it would end up, amid the glint of scalpels, the *snick* of blades sliding into flesh.

I was stuck in an in-between place, not sure whether I was in biology class or back at the School. Student voices and whitecoat voices bounced around in my mind.

Then Dr. Williams's face materialized all up in my grill. "Max, Dylan, how's it going so far?"

I nodded, trying to slow my breathing—I hadn't realized I'd been hyperventilating. "I'm okay...really." I looked up at his face, at the four wrinkles on his forehead, his almost calculating hazel eyes.

It was all somewhat...familiar.

Alarm bells went off in my head, wailing, *Danger danger danger!* My alarm bells were not to be taken lightly.

Was it possible that Dr. Williams was a whitecoat?

"Actually, I feel a bit sick," I said brusquely. "Come on, Dylan. Iggy!"

Iggy twitched on his stool and turned in the direction of my voice.

"C'mon, Ig," I repeated, ignoring Dylan's curious glance. "Time to go."

"Max, the boys seem fine," Dr. Williams said. Concerned or threatening, *concerned or threatening*? It was a question I had to ask myself way too often.

"No, I feel sick, too," Dylan said. *Good boy.*

Iggy wove through the maze of lab tables. "Gonna barf," he informed Dr. Williams. "Gotta go."

I strode toward the door, itching to hightail it out of there.

"Oh, no, you don't, Maximum," said Dr. Williams in a steely voice.

And here we go. I sighed.

I leaned forward onto the balls of my feet, ready to spring into action. Dylan moved ever so slightly, placing himself a bit in front of me and in a good fight position. I felt Iggy tense up. Tapping his forearm twice, I breathed, "Little over six feet. Bit of a belly. Dead center." Nobody but Iggy—and maybe Dylan—would be able to hear me. Ig inclined his chin the tiniest bit. He understood.

Dr. Williams shuffled past the cardboard box of chicken bags to his desk, where he brought out some Post-its and started scribbling. I watched him the entire time. If he charged, I'd drag Iggy and Dylan to the left, roll over the empty lab table, and shoot out the door. If he yanked a gun out of his geeky teacher pants, we'd dive behind the table, chuck some scalpels for good luck, and then shoot out the door.

"So what's the story, Doctor?" I asked Dr. Williams, crossing my arms. Everyone in the classroom was staring at us now. "Wait, I know—your plan is to make my life miserable? Or possibly destroy us?"

Dr. Williams smiled thinly. "What do you mean, Max? I just don't want you to get in trouble for walking out of class." He held out three hall passes.

Well, that was...unexpected. I narrowed my eyes at him, but he didn't falter.

"Let's go, boys." I shrugged and took the passes, and we walked out of the classroom.

My alarm bells never stopped ringing.

21

"MAX'S LIFE IS in danger."

Dylan's breath quickened. Okay, now Dr. Williams had his attention.

"But you can keep her safe, Dylan. All you have to do is cooperate with us."

After they'd fled the disastrous dissection lab, Dylan had realized that he'd left one of his textbooks behind, so he had gone back to get it.

Big mistake.

The other students were already gone, leaving only the biology teacher behind. Now Dylan was alone in the lab with him and the chicken carcasses, and it looked like he was, as Max would say, in deep, deep sneakers.

Dylan leaned against the table and frowned at the

teacher. "What do you want?" he said in a hostile voice he hoped sounded as tough as Max's. He fingered a scalpel that one of the other kids had left behind, but it didn't make him feel any more secure.

Dr. Williams smiled, making wrinkles appear around his mouth. "I'm not your enemy, Dylan. I have vital information for you, straight from Dr. Gunther-Hagen himself."

"That's impossible," Dylan said, his muscles tensing even more at the mention of the brilliant, diabolical man who had engineered his creation. The man who'd given him his life, and introduced him to Max. "Dr. Gunther-Hagen is dead."

"Oh, no, he's very much alive," promised Dr. Williams. "I've seen him myself."

Dylan stared at Dr. Williams but didn't respond. He had seen how Max looked at the biology teacher—with suspicion, distrust, and revulsion—and he didn't trust this man for an instant.

"And Dr. Gunther-Hagen has a special project for you," Dr. Williams continued. "A...mission, if you will."

"What sort of mission?" Dylan asked doubtfully.

"A mission it is vital you keep secret from Max if you value her safety." Dylan opened his mouth to protest, but Dr. Williams quickly cut him off. "It involves Fang."

Dylan shifted uncomfortably at the sound of the unwelcome name, feeling more and more boxed in among the stacks of laminated papers, bins of educational videos, dissection tools, and models of the various stages of mitosis.

"Fang is a far bigger threat than you realize—a bigger threat than any of us realized." Dr. Williams moved closer, seeming to delight in Dylan's discomfort. He watched him gravely. "I'm sharing this information with you because we know you are good, Dylan, that you can be trusted. We *can* trust you, can't we, Dylan?"

Dylan frowned. He did not like the turn this conversation was taking. Not at all. But at the mention of a secret, especially one about Fang, Dylan couldn't help leaning closer. His breath quickened.

"Fang's DNA, as it turns out, is different.... *Dangerous.* Dangerous in a way that bad people might use for their own selfish means. You wouldn't want to help the bad people, would you, Dylan?"

Dylan crossed his arms over his chest. "You can't expect me to buy this without an explanation."

As if to emphasize the delicacy of the information, in a hushed voice Dr. Williams described tests, experiments, and discoveries that boggled the mind. Dylan had certainly seen, felt, and heard about a lot of strange twists and turns of science in his few short years on the planet—not the least of which was being genetically enhanced to be able to heal wounds with his own saliva—but his mind was whirring a mile a minute at this strange, fascinating information he was learning about Fang's DNA. It could be the key to the most important medical discovery in human history....

But he wasn't even sure he believed it. And he definitely resented Dr. Williams's condescending tone.

"So you see, Dylan, it's very important that we *contain the threat*. That's where you come in. We need you to capture Fang, to *bring him to us*. You're stronger than Fang, Dylan," the doctor said, touching his arm. It was a compliment, but Dylan flinched. "Superior," the teacher continued. "You were *designed* for this. And you'd be doing a great service to the world, of course," he added, almost as an afterthought.

Dylan's eyes drifted to one of the chickens, still splayed open on the dissection table, its wings pinned open. They wanted to run more tests. On Fang. Dylan thought back to what Max had said about tests in her early life—about dog kennels and needles and whitecoats and drugs. He shook his head. Regardless of his history with Max's ex, and regardless of any threat Fang's DNA might pose, Dylan didn't hate him *that* much.

"No," Dylan said, already heading out of this room that was full of lies and bribes and the smell of formaldehyde. He didn't need to hear any more. "Find someone else to be your headhunter. You can tell Gunther-Hagen to stick his mission up his—"

"Ah, ah, ah," Dr. Williams interrupted before Dylan had reached the door. "One more little tidbit, Dylan," Dr. Williams called after him, holding up one finger. "If you don't accept this mission, well, we'll have to kill Max."

22

ANGEL'S EYES FLEW open and she gasped for air, scrabbling at the sides of her cage in terror. She took a slow, deep breath.

It was just a dream.

Angel slumped against the plastic wall of the dog crate, feeling icky and shaky and sore all over. In the time she'd been held captive, she had been electrified, operated on, beaten, scorched, and worked to exhaustion. But this nightmare was worse than any of it.

It hadn't been real...had it?

Every time she closed her eyes, images from the dream plastered the inside of her brain: Max, her neck covered in blood, dropping like a rock out of the sky...her brown eyes dulling with death as her skin grew pale...But Max wasn't dead, of course. Dead Max was the biggest oxymoron in history. Right?

Angel felt a rising panic. Her dreams, her visions, were almost never wrong. Except when she thought Fang would die. That hadn't happened . . . yet.

She bit her lip, staring at the roof of her cage through half-lidded eyes, trying to make a connection. And then, like an image appearing through the fog, Fang materialized.

Joy, pure and powerful, surged inside her—until Angel realized that Fang wasn't there. She was seeing him in another dreamlike vision. He was standing in a sea of red dust and blue sky, covered in blood and dirt and grime, but he didn't look like Fang, exactly. He looked ferocious and crazed, a mad dog about to attack. *Unhinged.*

"She's dead," Fang said, and Angel drew in a sharp breath, her whole body trembling. She hadn't dared to think it could really be true.

Fang's face twisted as he tried to control his anguish. He took a step toward two girls Angel recognized from Fang's gang: Star and Kate.

"Maya died because of you," he snarled.

Realization hit Angel like a ton of C4 bricks. Maya. Max II. Relief, and then horrible guilt, surged through her: Max was alive. It was *Maya* who was dead.

"We didn't know," Kate said, weeping, mascara running down her smooth brown cheeks. Kate was superstrong, Angel remembered, but she didn't look strong now. "Ari wasn't supposed to—" Her voice caught as she cried, but Fang's jaw was tensed, his features hard and calculating, his hands balled into fists.

Angel watched in dread. She knew that look. When crossed, Fang was deadly. *Get out of there*, she thought at the girls.

Star put an arm around her friend, and her usually harsh features softened. "We're sorry, Fang, but Maya... wasn't our fault. She was our friend."

Fang's laugh was harsh, his sneer horrifying. "Liar!" he shouted, towering over her. "Like I was your friend? You hated her," he spat, his eyes flashing.

Star shifted uncomfortably and tucked a stray piece of blond hair behind her ear, her elflike face tightening. "I never wanted her dead," she said quietly.

"Please, Fang," Kate hedged, sensing he was about to snap. "We were afraid. There's just too much danger following you. Jeb didn't tell us they'd try to kill—"

"How do you know Jeb?" Fang asked, his voice low and murderous. A vein pulsed in his temple as he absorbed the flare of shock at hearing Jeb Batchelder's name. Jeb, the man who'd once taken care of the flock like a father, but who'd turned out to be just another traitor. "How is he involved in this?"

"He said he'd keep us safe," Star shot back, her blue eyes accusing. "Which is more than you could do."

Fang's growl was fierce and guttural as he lunged for Star's throat like a wounded animal taking a last stand.

"Fang, don't!" Holden pleaded, his voice cracking.

Ratchet had grabbed Fang's arms. "Chill, man. Just chill. They're not worth it."

"You should know better than anyone that survival comes first," Star said smugly, but she cowered as Fang surged against Ratchet's grasp, gnashing his teeth.

Angel knew that Ratchet couldn't hold Fang back if he really wanted to kill Star and Kate. As angry as he was, he was *choosing* to spare them.

"Traitors!" Fang shrieked after the girls as they took off down the desert road. "Go on, run. Get out of my sight! If I ever see your faces again I'll tear you apart with my bare hands."

Then the vision ended, leaving Angel with the image of Fang's furious eyes, an ocean of hurt behind them. She blinked rapidly as the desert scene melted away, leaving her with a dull ache in her chest.

Max was alive, at least, but everything else seemed to be falling apart. Angel hunched into the emptiness of her dog crate, the thick smell of chemicals surrounding her and pain throbbing in every part of her body. She missed the flock so much.

If only Fang or Max were here with her.

23

"THAT IS MESSED up," Ratchet said angrily, standing over Fang. "You're not kicking us to the curb now, when we still gotta get back at that fanged freak. No way, man."

Fang nodded, staring into the smoldering embers of their campfire. He was aching all over, and his shirt was still covered in Maya's blood. "Sorry."

"Is this about Star and Kate?" Ratchet demanded. "You think we're like them? That I'd snitch? You *know* I don't roll like that." Even with his aggressive front, Fang could hear the real hurt in Ratchet's voice. "Look at these battle scars." Ratchet pulled up his sleeve, and his dark skin gleamed in the firelight. His arm was covered in slashes and bruises. "For *you*."

"It's not that," Fang said. "I just can't...do this. Besides

Star and Kate, Maya's dead, and...Look, there's nothing left. Fang's gang was a stupid fantasy. I'm just better on my own."

A fleeting thought of the flock made his chest tighten.

"No man is an island," Holden said with an awkward laugh, but Fang didn't react.

"Shut up, Starfish," Ratchet said halfheartedly, kicking an empty can into the darkness in frustration.

Holden brushed his sandy hair out of his face and pulled absentmindedly at the chunk of new skin on his earlobe, which had already grown back after one of the Erasers had bitten it off. After a minute, he said in a small voice, "Where are we supposed to go now?"

Fang sighed. "Go home."

"We don't have *homes* to go back to!" Ratchet exploded. "My guys saw me go off with you. You think they'll take me back? What've I got? *Nothing.*"

"I can't go back, either," Holden said softly. "My parents don't want me around. They're...they're *scared* of me."

"I know. I'm sorry. I don't know what to tell you." Fang pinched the bridge of his nose. He was exhausted. Maybe more exhausted than he'd ever been. He was tired of making plans, of solving problems. He didn't know how Max had stood it for so long. "You'll figure it out."

"So that's it." Ratchet's voice was cold. "After all we've been through, you're just saying, 'So long, it's been fun'?"

"Sorry," said Fang. "But it actually hasn't been that fun." And then he stood up and limped away into the desert night.

24

COOL FINGERS PRESSED against Angel's forehead. Someone was taking the bandages off her eyes.

She didn't even struggle; she just lay there limply. There
was no point fighting it anymore.

"Hey, sweetie," the someone said, and Angel gasped—
she knew that voice. She'd heard that voice so many times.

Jeb.

Jeb here, in the School, taking off the bandages from
the operation.

"*You.*" Angel cringed away from his hands, fury cours-
ing through her. "Don't touch me!" she spat. "You deserted
us. Again. I'm here because of *you.*"

"I know, sweetheart," Jeb said. "I'm so sorry, Angel. I

can't explain to you how sorry I am. You have to let me explain—"

"No," Angel growled, and felt his hands twitch; he was startled. "I don't care. You don't get to explain after *this*." She touched her tender face.

"Sweetheart..."

"Don't call me that ever again," she cried. "I said I don't care—I don't care about any of it. About your excuses. About you. About the rest of the human race." She was seething, and her voice was harsh and icy even to her own ears. "All people do is hurt one another," she continued bitterly. "So let them all die. Let the doomsday, or whatever they're calling it now, happen. *I don't care*."

Jeb brushed her dirty hair away from her face, her curls damp with sweat, but Angel clawed at his fingers. "Angel, please listen to me. I'll make everything okay again, no one will hurt you—"

"*I said shut up!*" she shrieked. Her small body was shaking. "You just couldn't stop at Iggy, could you, Jeb?"

"What do you mean?" Jeb asked. He sounded on the verge of horror.

"What do you think I mean?" asked Angel, her voice rising with hysteria. She felt clumsily for the sides of her cage. "I'm *blind*."

25

FANG LEANED AGAINST the cold, rough tombstone.

It was twilight, and the sky above the graveyard was a pale indigo. The trees rustled with a slight breeze, but no birds sang, no crickets chirped. Fang was completely alone.

Blood trickled slowly from the wound on his wing, where the bone had cracked and punctured the skin as he'd flown up to catch Maya. At the time, he hadn't even noticed the pain. It was pulsing dully now, and he was letting it bleed.

Pain from somewhere other than his heart was a welcome change.

He deserved the pain, Fang told himself. Everything was his fault.

If he had paid more attention in that battle with the

henchgoons, if he had kept tabs on Maya the entire time, she wouldn't have fought Ari in the air. She wouldn't have died in Fang's arms. She would still be alive today, warm and happy and Maxish and not Maxish, having his back when things got too real.

Fang stared up at the moon, only barely visible in the murky dusk. Things had gotten too real.

First Angel. Then Maya. Both innocent, both dead.

All his fault.

He was a murderer.

He let his head drop into his hands, and shut his eyes tight. At least Ratchet and Holden were okay now—without Fang and the danger that came with him, they'd be all right. Fang could not be trusted as a leader; that much was horribly obvious. How could he save the world if he couldn't even protect the few people he loved?

Swallowing, Fang looked up, around the graveyard. Tombstone after tombstone, death after death, epitaph after epitaph, summing up a life, or a worldview, in a few words. What would his gravestone say, he wondered, assuming he wasn't left to rot in the open air?

FANG: GREW UP IN A DOG CRATE. FELL IN LOVE. SCREWED IT UP. FAILED AT LIFE.

Wait a second. Something caught his eye.

Fang scrambled to his feet and crossed to the tombstone that read JULIE EVANS, 1955–2010 in two strides. He knelt before it, reaching out and tracing the epitaph.

YOU HAVEN'T FAILED UNTIL YOU QUIT TRYING.

A sign from the universe? Fang's brain being so pathetic that it was making up coincidences?

Either way, he *couldn't* quit yet. Fang had a role in this—whatever it was—and now that he'd lost two people, he wouldn't lose any more.

Fang touched the engraved words one more time, then kicked off from the grass and soared into the darkening sky.

26

FANG STARED AT his warped, distorted reflection.

He was standing in Millennium Park, Chicago, in front of the huge stainless-steel sculpture nicknamed "The Bean." Around his reflection curved the city skyline, clear blue sky and tall majestic buildings. This place was one of the many stops he'd made in the past few days. He was newly motivated, as if the words on the gravestone had injected him with pure determination.

Fang was trying to understand the 99% Plan.

His wing was still messed up, so he'd taken buses and trains—had even hitchhiked—all over the country, from South Florida, thick with gray fog, to the smooth golden plains of Oklahoma. He had seen the vivid colors of the

Arizona sunset. He had watched small waves lap the shores of Lake Erie.

Every place he had visited had held rumors and evidence. All over America, people were stirring restlessly in anticipation. You could feel the energy in the air, building to the breaking point. It was like the calm before the storm.

But this was not a storm of revolution, like so many others in history. This was a darker, more violent storm—twisted, raging. It was a storm of desolation.

There had been dozens of demonstrations, some of which turned into senseless riots. Celebrities were updating their Twitter profiles en masse, writing things like "Earth is mine, 1 more for 99." Slack-jawed Plan members were milling around outside hospital maternity wards wearing sheets scrawled with such slogans as LESS IS MORE. END REPRODUCTION NOW. The brutal stoning of a homeless amputee ("the Plan does not allow for the weak") was just one example of the escalating violence.

There were large meetings in every city, held in universities and government buildings, in which "rational" lectures were led by smiling, serenely confident "experts," discussing the benefits of "selection." All of which, to Fang's utter disgust, the news outlets covered with a mix of excited panic and restrained approval.

They wouldn't be so approving, Fang thought, *if they really understood the extent of the 99% Plan.* Because through eavesdropping—and, okay, a couple of bribes—Fang had confirmed what he'd feared: These people, the remnants of the Doomsday Group and the By-Half Plan, wanted to reduce the earth to only the enhanced.

That is, to exterminate the human race.

Fang shook his head in revulsion, still unable to comprehend it. The same crazies from the past had somehow become *even crazier*. That was no surprise.

But the American people were actually going along with it.

Fang's fists clenched as he thought of all of the places he'd seen, the millions of people struggling through their individual lives, their loves....

All that beauty.

All that history.

And all these people, so eager to destroy it.

Book Two

AND SO
IT BEGINS

27

ANGEL HEARD JEB'S breath catch in horror.

"They didn't," he said hollowly. "Not you, too. Not your eyes."

"You're just upset because you wrecked your perfect little specimen," Angel spat, shoving away his hands and retreating farther into her dog crate. She still ached all over.

Jeb clutched the door of the cage, shuddering so hard that he rattled the metal grid. "Oh, Angel..."

"Save it."

"It's like Ari all over again," he said brokenly. "So many failures...so many mistakes. You can't imagine the remorse I feel, Angel...."

It's your own fault, Angel thought, but she was almost

surprised to hear tears in his voice. She couldn't remember Jeb ever crying, no matter what happened.

"I was such a bad father to him," continued Jeb dejectedly.

Angel bristled. Ari had been a disaster, that was for sure, but he was dead. Angel was the one who was here; *she* was the one whose eyes had been ruined. His apology had been meaningless, but this little heart-to-heart about Ari was straight-up insulting.

And he wouldn't shut up. "After Ari died, I just...I had to try again. I had to give myself another chance at being a father, at caring for a son. That's why I worked so closely with Dr. Gunther-Hagen."

Wait, what? Angel sat up straight inside her crate, her attention snapping back to Jeb. She forgot her anger for a moment. "You were creating another Ari?"

"I swore this time I wouldn't fail. I would be a good father...." Jeb's voice caught in his throat. "And he would be a good son. I would retire from my work with the School and care for him with all my heart."

And despite *everything*, Angel couldn't help but feel the tiniest twinge of pity. Here Jeb was, a fully grown man, sobbing over his dead son.

"You have to understand, Angel," Jeb pleaded. "I had only the best in mind. Just one new Ari. Then it would end."

"But it didn't end," Angel whispered, thinking of the flying mutants they'd battled for months.

"Well, of course there were many less-than-perfect

attempts," Jeb conceded. "But Dr. Gunther-Hagen is an incredibly brilliant geneticist. With his help, I made Ari bigger and better than ever before, seamless and strong. Finally, I had my son back." Jeb wasn't crying anymore. He sounded almost triumphant.

Triumphant, and something else.

Angel felt the dread building in her stomach.

"The not-Aris were useful, too," Jeb said. "Not as sons, but as warriors, designed for one mission, and one mission only."

"Mission?"

When he spoke, Angel could hear the cold serenity in his tone. "To eliminate Fang."

28

"WHAT?" ANGEL FELT her skull prickle all over and her hands go numb. The air around her felt like it was vibrating, and she rested her head against the plastic wall of the dog crate, breathing deeply.

With darkness consuming her vision, she couldn't see Jeb's face, but she could picture it clearly: the laugh lines around his mouth, a bit of stubble on his jawline, and his eyes—intelligent eyes that she had once known so well, that she had trusted, that even Max had trusted. The eyes that seemed well meaning, even when he was screwing everything up.

She must've misunderstood him.

"Wait—*what?*" she said again, shaking her head to clear it. "Eliminate Fang...as in, *kill Fang?*"

"That's what the 99% Plan is all about," Jeb said simply.

He sounded calm. Creepily, eerily calm. The calm that comes with absolute certainty. It was terrifying.

"Isn't 99% about *sparing* the mutants?" Angel tried to keep her voice as calm as Jeb's, though her body was shaking all over. "How can that mean killing Fang?"

"It's about the good of the planet versus the good of the people, Angel," he explained in an indulgent tone, as if they were talking about why she needed to share with others or conserve water. "You know I love Fang like another son." It was true—she had thought he did. Angel instantly regretted pitying him earlier.

"Then how could you do this?" Angel asked, her voice rising. "I'll forgive you, Jeb," she said suddenly. She touched her eyelids again, choking back tears. "I'll forgive you, and everything that happened with Ari won't matter anymore. You can turn it all around. Just don't do this." She was gripping the bars of her cage, pleading with him.

Jeb was silent for so long that Angel held her breath, a twinge of hope swelling in her.

Then he sighed heavily. "No. He's too dangerous now. If he remains alive, his life will become a living hell."

"But *why*?" Angel demanded.

"Hans will see to it. Remember back in Dr. Gunther-Hagen's lab, when Fang almost died?"

She nodded. It was one of her worst memories, even worse than the ones from when she was really little, in the School.

"As a result of those tests, Hans has recently discovered something *truly extraordinary* about Fang's DNA."

"What kind of discovery?" Angel asked bleakly. Jeb had no answers, no explanations—only more vague justifications. She felt empty.

"Something amazing," Jeb replied with such bright enthusiasm that Angel wanted to hit him. They were talking about the reason for Fang's *death*. "Something that would change the world."

Suddenly, the soft padding sound of footsteps reached Angel's ears. Someone was coming toward them.

"Yes, Angel, something that would change the world," a cool female voice said. "And now we need to find out if you, sweetie, have the same... *defect*."

Angel felt like she was going to throw up.

She knew that voice.

Dr. Martinez, Max's mom, was at the School.

29

"REMEMBER, FIRST IMPRESSIONS are *key*," Total told me sagely.

I stared. "Total, there is no first impression. I've been *living* with the guy for like three months, for Pete's sake."

He flapped his little black wings and sniffed. "Well, *excuse me* for trying to help with your—might I remind you—first-ever date with Dylan."

Rolling my eyes, I attempted to get a brush through my ratty hair for the umpteenth time. "It's not even a date." I sighed. "Dylan and I are *chaperoning* Nudge and Sloan."

"I bet Nudge would accept my advice graciously."

"Perfect! So go talk to Nudge, then!"

Total whined. "But unlike you, she already knows the

ins and outs of being a normal teenager. You're the dys-functional one here."

I scowled. "Fine. Give me advice."

"Ask nicely."

"*Total.*"

"Sheesh, no need to get all snippy," he said, pouting as effectively as a Scottish terrier can pout. "Just remember: No one likes a self-absorbed person. Always direct the conversation back to your date."

"I already know everything about my . . . about Dylan," I said. I sighed again and wound my hair into a lopsided bun, then tried to jam in a couple of the chopstick-y things that Nudge uses for her hair. Welcome to the glamorous life of Maximum Ride, ladies and gentlemen.

"Also, personal hygiene is a *must*," Total continued.

We both looked at my messy hair, my stained jeans, my beat-up sneakers.

"I'll get Nudge to choose an outfit for you," he muttered.

I stared at my reflection in the mirror, trying not to panic. Do I need to repeat how awful I am at this—this normal girl stuff? No. I don't believe I do.

But Sloan was a fifteen-year-old boy. I don't care how nice the guy might be, that's a walking hormonal disaster waiting to happen, in my book. There was no way I was just going to sit there and let him whisk Nudge away by herself, so to keep it from being horribly awkward, Dylan and I were double-*whatevering* with them.

Kill me now.

"So what movie are you crazy kids seeing, anyway?" Total asked fondly.

"*Blood City III: The Massacre.*" I'd read the summary of it online, and frankly, it sounded like the directors had just decided to film my life.

"Perfect!" Total crowed, wagging his tail. "A horror movie! You can cling to Dylan during all the scary parts."

Flabbergasted, I gaped at him. "First of all, sexist pig much?" I said. "I don't buy into the whole damsel-in-distress thing, especially when I've saved Dylan's feathery butt more times than he can count. Second of all, no. Just…no."

Total ignored me and hopped up onto the counter and opened the medicine cabinet with his nose, taking out a little white box and pushing it toward me.

"What's that?" I asked warily.

Total winked. "Breath mints."

30

"NOOOO!" ON THE screen, a woman's eyes bugged almost out of her head, and I tried not to scream.

Tried not to scream in exasperation, I mean. The serial killer was right in front of her, wide open! Clearly, instead of weeping like a moron, she should be lunging forward and administering a swift uppercut to his chin. Then this entire pointless ordeal would be over with, and I could go home.

Okay. I'll stop whining. It wasn't *that* bad, sitting there in the movie theater next to Dylan. We were in the row directly behind Nudge and Sloan—partly so we wouldn't get separated, partly so I could knock Sloan unconscious if he tried anything—and, to be completely honest, I was feeling pretty relaxed.

In a completely nervous, freaked-out way, of course.

Because as soon as the words AND NOW…YOUR FEATURE PRESENTATION had flickered across the screen, Dylan had tentatively reached out and taken my hand.

And I hadn't stopped him.

So that was the situation: dark theater, warm hands, terrible blood-drenched movie, and so much tension between me and Dylan that it felt like my brain was about to short-circuit.

Basically, I wasn't sure whether to just go with it and have fun (like a human) or panic and get the heck out of this pitch-black enclosed space (like a bird kid). So far, the human way was winning, but the jury was still out.

To absolutely no one's surprise, the stupid bug-eyed lady got stabbed, and wailed dramatically. I turned to the side and made a face at Dylan.

"Well, you can't blame her," he whispered, and his eyes flashed like blue coins in the dim half-light. "She hasn't exactly been trained for fights to the death."

"Oh, come on! She still totally just sat there and let herself get stabbed," I protested. "In my humble opinion, she deserved it."

He snickered quietly. "You may be the only person who's rooting for the serial killer."

We smiled at each other, and that was when my usual harshness came slamming back into me with a jolt, making me bite my lip and focus on the movie again. *No time for blushing and admiring; make sure Nudge is doing okay! Check for escape routes!*

Sometimes my survival skills really get in the way of things.

I stayed completely still through the rest of the movie, even when Dylan's thumb began tracing fiery circles on my palm, even when my heart started pounding so loudly I thought people six rows away could probably hear it. *Get it together*, I told myself. *Be calm. Be Zen. You are Buddha.*

Except I highly doubt that Buddha would be experiencing the same tingles down his spine that I was. And because of Dylan! *Someone, anyone, just put me in a straitjacket and be done with it.*

Finally, the screen went black and the end credits started rolling. I shot to my feet, dropping Dylan's hand like a hot potato. "Okay, well, that was fun! Let's head home now!"

"No way," Nudge said, frowning. "It's only nine o'clock."

"Yeah," said Sloan. He nudged Nudge—no pun intended—and gave her a little smirk. "Let's you and me go back to my place."

I choked, not sure whether to be horrified or revolted or amused. For one thing, if this guy thought there was even a *slim* chance that I'd let him get his hands all over my Nudge, he was sorely mistaken. For another thing, gross. For a third thing, what "place"? Didn't this kid have *parents*? I mean, true, *we* didn't, but we weren't exactly the norm.

"No, I think we'll be going home now," I growled, grabbing Dylan's wrist and practically pushing him out into the aisle. "C'mon, Nudge."

Nudge sulked, but she followed obediently, with a glowering Sloan right behind her. He probably hated me, which I cared absolutely zero about. He wouldn't be the first one.

As soon as we stepped out of the theater and into the cool night air, I let out a sigh of relief. No matter how many amazingly attractive guys held my hand, no matter how many dates I went on, I would always, *always* prefer to be out in open space, with room for flying.

Unless, of course, that space was filled with three hulking figures.

"We've been waiting for you guys," said Ari.

31

FOR A FEW moments, I couldn't even speak. All I could do was stare dumbly at the person who'd died in my arms. *Twice.*

Ari.

And he wasn't alone. Two big, snarling Erasers flanked him, looking oddly similar to their ringleader.

"How are you...*alive?*" I asked shakily. Sloan visibly tensed at my words, and I remembered that, while undoubtedly a sleazy moron, he was still a relatively innocent human. If this turned into a fight, it would be bad.

"I'm not a zombie," Ari said in his gruff voice. "Just a better version of myself."

I tensed, my hands twitching. The previous versions hadn't been particularly pleasant.

Ari chuckled. "Don't look so nervous, Max. I didn't come on this friendly little visit to see you, anyway." He looked pointedly at Dylan. "'Sup, Dyl."

"Do I know you?" Dylan cocked his head, confused and understandably wary. "Max? Who is this?"

This weird man-wolf-child? I didn't really know how to answer that. Ari and I had been mortal enemies—his first death had been caused by me accidentally breaking his neck in a New York subway tunnel—and then we'd been kind of friends. And then he'd died. What was I supposed to make of this new Ari?

When in doubt, play it safe. I narrowed my eyes. "Yes, Ari, tell us. Who are you this time? Good? Evil? Still deciding?"

"Relaaax, sis. We're buds. My third coming is in peace. Actually, I already did you a favor." His wolfy grin just sent more adrenaline hurtling through me.

"What kind of favor?"

Ari crossed his arms proudly. "I killed your clone."

"*Clone?*" Sloan said shrilly, but we all ignored him.

My stomach clenched. "You what?" I snarled, but I knew it was true even before Ari elaborated.

"'Fraid so," he said, smirking. "A scratch, a smash, wham, bam, Max II is dead—just like you always wanted."

I swallowed. Admittedly, I'd flirted with the idea, but not for *real*.

"Anyway, on to business," Ari said lightly before I could respond. He looked again at Dylan, who, taking a cue from me, had assumed a hostile stance. "Jeb wanted me to tell you not to worry about Dr. G.-H. and your little mission."

"Jeb?" Dylan asked, clearly confused.

"Jeb!" I exclaimed, my voice rising. "What does Jeb have to do with—"

"We've got the situation covered," Ari said with finality, his eyes boring into Dylan's. I scowled. His smile was playful, but in his eyes there was a definite threat.

"What does he mean, Dylan?" I demanded impatiently.

Dylan shook his head, but he adjusted his stance almost imperceptibly. He seemed to be deciding whether or not to spring.

"Someone had better tell me what's going on," I snapped, ready to fight both of them. *"Now."*

"What I mean is that I'll be defanging your buddy Fang." Ari finally looked at me, smiling cheerfully.

Nudge gasped.

"What?" I exclaimed, heat rising to my cheeks even as my blood ran cold.

"And I just stopped by to make sure I wouldn't have to add Dylan to the list while I'm at it," Ari continued calmly. "Maxy here can tell you I'm a bit hard to keep down." He flashed a conspiratorial grin. "So cease and desist, bud. Cease and desist."

We all regarded one another suspiciously, and I tensed with growing fury and confusion. Ari wanted to kill Fang? And he was warning Dylan about it, even though Dylan *hated* Fang? And somehow Jeb was involved?

"Who's this Fang guy, and what do you mean, 'defang'?" Sloan asked nervously, a little slow on the uptake. "Like, you're gonna knock his teeth out?"

Ari turned toward him and cracked his knuckles.

"Naw, kid," he said. "I mean like I'm gonna tear his heart out through his chest."

"That's it," I snapped, but as I lunged forward, Ari and his posse unfurled their wings, as if choreographed, and kicked off from the ground, hard.

I began to shrug off my jacket to do the same, but Dylan reached out and put his hand on my shoulder.

"You can't take him right now," Dylan murmured in my ear. "Too many people around."

I eyed Sloan, who was stammering "Wh-what the…" next to a horrified Nudge, along with a small group of onlookers who were pointing and taking pictures.

I ground my teeth, but nodded and took a deep breath, unclenching my fists. Fang could take care of himself, I reminded myself. He'd be *fine*.

"Nice chatting with you guys," called Ari from above. "Remember what I said, Dylan. Cease and desist."

And with that, he rose into the darkness and was gone.

32

I WAS JUST rolling into my third hour of sleeplessness when the door to my room creaked open.

I was on guard instantly, bolting upright and wrapping one hand around my bedside lamp. Sound extreme? Not when you've been ambushed in your sleep as many times as I have.

"Who's there?" I whispered. "Nudge?" She had been utterly devastated over stupid Sloan, crying for at least forty minutes after he had called her a freak and hightailed it out of the parking lot. I wouldn't be surprised if she wanted yet more comforting. Even if I wasn't necessarily the best comforter in the world.

"No, it's me." Very recognizable voice. Completely unexplainable, what he was doing here, but recognizable.

I put the lamp down and flicked it on. Standing in the doorway was Dylan, looking tired and rumpled and sheepish.

"What the heck are you doing in my room?" I asked, incredulous. "It's past midnight. I'm *sleeping.*" *Well, trying to.*

We hadn't talked after Ari's little visit. I'd been too freaked out by his news about Fang, and too preoccupied with Nudge's tears, and then I'd stalked off to my room to try to make sense of things. No luck there.

Dylan shuffled awkwardly. "I...was wondering...if there was any way I could...stay in here tonight." He mumbled the last words, but I still got them.

I made a sound reminiscent of a dying cat. *"What?"*

"I hate being alone at night," he muttered while I gaped. "I know it's stupid and lame, but I mean—I'm not like you. I haven't been alive for fifteen years."

The truth of that statement hit me harder than it should have. It was just so easy to forget that Dylan had been created only two years ago when he looked my age.

"A lot's been happening lately," he went on in a rush. "Usually I'd just deal with it, but it's a lot to absorb, and I was lying there in bed thinking about all the screwed-up things that Ari guy said, and...I don't know." Yeah, sounded a bit like my evening.

He looked up at me hopefully. "So can I stay in here? Just for tonight? On the floor or something."

I hesitated a second more, then sighed heavily and gave a tiny nod.

Relief crossed his male-model face. He came in, dragging his quilt behind him like a little kid, and closed the door quietly. "Thanks." He looked embarrassed to be needing something, to be this vulnerable. I could have eviscerated him just then, but I hadn't.

Because I am a freaking *princess* about other people's feelings.

"No prob," I said. "Pull up a patch of floor."

He shook the quilt out and lay down with a lithe grace, his smooth muscles rippling. I swallowed, trying not to think of how those arms had brushed against mine in the theater. He tucked his wings behind him as he lay on his side—none of us were back sleepers, for obvious reasons. With one hand he reached back and pulled the quilt over him.

He looked big and strong and vulnerable and really, really . . . appealing.

I flicked off the light and threw my pillow down to him. It landed on his face.

"Thanks," he said again, pulling the pillow off and bunching it up under his head. "This is just for tonight."

"Better be," I muttered, then drifted back to the thoughts that had been eating away at me. Everything that Ari had said had been growing larger in the quiet of the night.

"Dylan?" I said after a few minutes.

"Hmm?"

"What did Ari mean, about 'cease and desist'? Why

would he come looking for you if you'd never even met him before?"

Dylan didn't answer for such a long time that I thought he'd fallen asleep. Finally, he sighed. "I don't understand any of it. I never understand why anyone involves me in anything."

I rolled my eyes. I had little patience for self-pity, and if I'd had another pillow, I would've chucked that at him, too.

"He said not to worry about Dr. Gunther-Hagen," I pressed, my voice sounding small and shrill in my ears. "Maybe he meant you shouldn't worry about being my perfect other half, like Hansy said. Maybe he meant you should stop pursuing me."

"Maybe," he said quietly, and my heart thundered in my chest. I was glad I couldn't see his face in the darkness. "But I can't, Max. You know I can't."

We were quiet again, each of us listening to the other's breathing. Finally, Dylan exhaled, long and slow. "Good night, Max."

I stared at the ceiling, willing my thoughts away from his body, his breath. "Good night, Dylan."

33

FANG	DYLAN
Knows me better than anyone (both a positive and a negative).	Practically just met me (less blackmail material).
Can completely trust him (probably).	Seems trustworthy (so far).
Helps me stay tough.	Helps me admit I can't always be tough.

FANG	DYLAN
Doesn't care about social skills. Like me.	A freaking social butterfly. Complements my antisocial behavior.
Has eyes that seem to see inside me. Not good.	Has eyes that make me forget myself. Not good.
Is capable of bringing the meaning of "irritating" to whole new levels.	Is capable of... pretty much the same thing.
Almost like a brother (ack).	Not like a brother. At all. In any way.
Closed off.	Makes darn sure that I know every single emotion going through his head.
I don't know how to act around him anymore.	Easy to be around.

FANG	DYLAN
Never told me he loved me. (Writing it in a letter right before he deserted me doesn't count. Coward.)	Loves me. And told me so. Right to my face. Gulp.
Intense. Powerful. Moves in a way that makes me ache to touch him.	Strong. Beautiful. Looks at me in a way that makes me ache to...scratch that.
Still having dreams about the way he kissed me.	Ditto.
Don't know where he is right now. Because he freaking left.	Is right here with me. Now. Always.

IT WAS A pretty complete list. The kind of list one makes when one cannot fall asleep because one's thoughts keep swirling through one's brain like a bunch of sparrows on crack. I put down my notebook, rolled over, and gazed at the floor.

Dylan had rolled over onto his other side and was facing the opposite wall, his quilt balled up at his feet. He was a turbulent sleeper. Unlike Fang, who was quiet and self-contained. I started to add that to the list, but then thought, *Who cares?*

I frowned at Dylan's sprawled limbs. He couldn't possibly be comfortable. He was probably cold.

"Hey...you cold down there?" I whispered, leaning over the edge of the bed.

He didn't answer. Seeing as how he was asleep and all. I watched his breathing, slow and steady, the shadow of his abdominal muscles rising and falling under his bunched-up T-shirt. I tried to slow my own breath, but it thundered quick and ragged in my ears.

Before I knew what I was doing, I was out of bed with my own comforter. I felt sorry for him. Yeah, that was it. Really sorry for him. As anyone would.

The floor was freezing against my bare feet. I padded over to Dylan and carefully lay down next to him. He shifted, coughing, and I froze. After two long minutes, satisfied that he was still asleep, I curled myself into him, drawing my comforter over us both. I felt the warmth of his body against mine, his breath on the back of my neck, making the tiny hairs rise.

We fit like two puzzle pieces. Just like we were supposed to. The whole designed-to-be-my-perfect-other-half thing...

Gah.

But you know what? Just this once, I was going to shove away all my angst and confusion and fear and just focus on the present.

Which happened to be very warm. Maddeningly warm. My whole body felt tingly.

With that thought in mind, I pressed myself closer against Dylan's sleeping form and closed my eyes, drifting into the sweetest sleep I'd had in a long, long time.

I wasn't sure I ever wanted to wake up.

34

THE NEXT DAY at school was, predictably, a complete horror show.

Not for me (for once), but for Nudge, who'd been publicly spurned and ridiculed by Sloan, in front of all of the popular girls. In less than a minute, this new gossip was all over Facebook and Twitter.

About eight hours later I was rapping my knuckles against the door to Nudge's room. As soon as we'd gotten home from school she had gone in there and locked the door behind her, and she didn't come out for dinner. I couldn't blame her—things had only gotten worse after Sloan's scaredy-cat retreat.

God, I should've unleashed a can of whup-ass on him.

"Nudge? Come on, open the door. Let's make popcorn."

"Go away," came Nudge's weak voice. "Don't wanna talk about it."

"We don't have to talk about it," I said. *Please, no—no more talking about it, I beg you.* "I just want to make sure you're okay. Open up, will you? We can make hot chocolate."

After a few moments of silence, I heard her trudge across the room. The door opened.

Nudge's face was stained with the tears she'd been holding in all day; rivers of mascara ran down her cheeks. Her big brown eyes were puffy and bloodshot.

I had no idea what to do. I'd already offered popcorn and hot chocolate. What else was there?

"It's just getting worse and worse," moaned Nudge. "First it was just stupid gossip. Now I'm an outcast. They all think I'm some kind of circus sideshow. As usual."

"Come here," I murmured, putting my arms around her. "I know it's a drag to have everyone at school treat us like lepers"—to put it mildly—"but they're just gullible, prejudiced jerks. Typical Avian-American prejudice." I eased her head onto my shoulder, which I should have lined with paper towels first. "I'm really sorry Sloan was such a butt-head," I said soothingly. "But sweetie, he's so unworthy. You deserve better than that. You deserve someone who's going to love you, wings and all."

I'd hardly ever seen such sadness on her face. "That's easy for you to say. You have *two* guys who love you." She looked up at me, and I didn't know what to say to her. "I don't have *anyone*."

I swallowed nervously. Guiltily.

"That's not true. You have *us*," I blurted out, knowing full well how lame that was. The flock was awesome and all, but it just can't be compared to the rapture of being loved, held, adored. In that... *different* way.

I quickly shook off the pleasurable shiver that shot down my spine as I remembered spending the night on the floor next to Dylan.

"Listen. Soon we'll blow this Popsicle stand and move on, and then you'll never have to deal with any of them ever again. Until we get rich and famous, and then you can have fun spurning them when they beg for your autograph." I smiled, pulling her close, but Nudge wasn't amused.

"I don't *want* to move on," she cried, pulling out of my arms. "Can't you see that? I don't want to 'spurn' them!" She made air quotes with her fingers, glaring at me. How had I become the enemy here, exactly? "I just want to—" Her voice broke, and she drew in a trembling breath. "I just want to be *liked* by them, Max!" And then Nudge burst into tears. Again. Crap.

"Oh, sweetie," I said helplessly, uncomprehending. I had spent very little energy in my life trying to be liked by anyone. "Come here. Come sit down," I said, taking her hand and tugging her toward the bed.

Then I saw that the entire thing was covered with crumpled-up pieces of paper. A pair of scissors was lying on top of a stack of teen magazines, all of which had been mangled and cut to pieces.

"Nudge? What's this?"

Nudge blew her nose miserably and gestured at a pile of blocky, badly cutout shapes. "Those are for my scrapbook."

I picked up one of the shapes. It was a photo of a pretty teenage model, smiling brightly at the camera, wearing some sort of sparkly outfit with furry boots. "Blech," I said, and put the photo down. The next photo was another pretty model. So was the next one. And the next.

"What kind of scrapbook are you making, exactly?" I asked Nudge cautiously.

Her bottom lip quivered. "I want to be like them. Like those girls."

I raised my eyebrows. "You want to be a model?"

"No." She sighed dramatically, rolling her eyes. "I want to not be a *freak*."

"Nudge, normal is way overrated...." I began. Déjà vu.

"Oh, yeah, it's superlame to just want to have friends, to just want to be kissed, like everyone else." She laughed bitterly. "You sound like the whitecoats. Being lab experiments doesn't make us better, Max. We aren't *enhanced*, we're *mutants*."

Wow. I had to remind myself that this was not the sweet Nudge I knew. This was a love-scorned girl who had just been through a day of despicable bullying. I was lucky she wasn't actually breathing fire.

"And if we were normal, there wouldn't be people trying to kill us," she pointed out.

"Well, probably," I admitted. "But I *guarantee* you people at school would still do mean things to nice kids for no reason. That's just the way life works."

Nudge shook her head. "No. You know what? There's only one answer to all our problems."

This didn't sound good. "What is it?" I asked warily.

She snatched the scissors off the bed and looked so utterly reckless that it sent me into a panic.

"Nudge!" I gasped.

But Nudge turned from me and eyed a poster on the wall—a publicity poster of the whole flock, from our days as a flying sideshow—and then, lightning-quick, she let the scissors fly with as much skill and fury as she'd displayed battling Erasers. With a hollow thud, the blades struck the image of Nudge's wing and embedded themselves deep in the wall.

I swallowed, my throat suddenly dry. My own wings twitched under my shirt.

Then she clutched one of her normal-girl photos to her chest, her eyes fierce with determination. "The only answer to all our problems is getting rid of our wings," she said. "Removing them forever. I'm gonna do it someday, Max. I swear it."

35

FANG OPENED HIS eyes blearily. Above him was nothing but the clear night sky, dotted with millions of tiny glittering stars. It was beautiful.

It was quiet and calm, and yet for some reason he'd woken up.

He sat up, quickly scanning his surroundings for anything threatening, anything that might have made some sort of noise.

Nothing.

He still found it weird, nowadays, to wake up alone. Until this past year, waking up had always meant being flung into the noise and chaos of the flock.

The flock. Fang had thought that it would get easier, being away from them, as time went on. He'd thought wrong. He'd thought that they'd be fine—even better off—without him, and that it would be easier for him to pursue whatever mission he had if he didn't have to worry about them. Now he wasn't sure.

And then there was the gang. Fang sighed and lay back down, making hardly a sound on the dew-dampened grass. Why had he ever thought that would work? Why had he tried? The gang had gotten Maya *killed*.

Fang swallowed and closed his eyes. Maya was dead. And though Ari kept demonstrating a freaky, jack-in-the-box ability to come back from the dead, Fang was pretty sure Maya was gone for good.

And the others—he'd really let them down. Fang frowned and pulled his jacket tighter around himself, turning onto his other side. He wasn't used to letting people down. He was used to coming through for people. He'd thought being on his own meant that he could make all the decisions by himself, that he didn't need to rely on Max to do all the thinking. The bad thing was that he had no one to discuss decisions with, no one to bounce ideas off of.

Admit it, you idiot—it's more than that. You miss her, Fang thought.

He sighed and rolled onto his back, restless. He was exhausted, thinking about it all. But not exhausted enough to fall back to sleep.

She doesn't need you, he reminded himself. *She has the Winged Wonder by her side. Maybe being on your own is just too hard?*

No, he couldn't think tha—

Fang.

Fang jerked, startled, and peered into the dark trees and shrubs around him.

Fang, nobody's there.

Oh, man. The voice—or rather Voice—wasn't coming from around him.

It was coming from *inside* him.

Not again. He had to wonder—was this the same Voice Max got? Where did it come from? Why was it appearing in his brain *now*? Sure, all of them had heard the Voice at one time or another. But Fang definitely didn't want this to become an everyday thing.

Okay, what is it? Fang thought. *What do you want?*

It's time to go, Fang, the Voice replied. *She does need you now, more than ever.*

Who needs me? he asked, but he already knew the answer.

Go home to Max.

36

"IS SHE IN trouble? Are the others okay?" Fang demanded aloud, sitting up, alone in the darkness. *What's going on?* he screamed inside his head.

But the Voice stayed silent, in that incredibly annoying way it had. It was gone. For how long, he didn't know.

Go home to Max.

He had no idea if something was really wrong, but he couldn't exactly ignore the Voice, either. When Max heard her Voice, she pretty much always listened to it. His Voice was saying that Max needed him more than ever.

He pretended he didn't feel the way his heart was speeding up with excitement and anxiety, just thinking about going back.

No doubt his replacement would still be there, being all

Dylan-rific and glaring at Fang with narrowed eyes. Well, too bad. What choice did Fang have? None. He would've liked to have just taken off right then, raced back to the flock. To Max. To see that she was all right. But Fang's wing had been bothering him more and more, and he definitely wasn't in flying shape yet.

So he'd be patient. He'd find the nearest town and then get on the Internet. He would do some research before he went racing back to the person he kept trying to leave.

Two hours later the sun was just beginning to rise, and Fang was seated at a computer in an Internet cafe. He sipped from a Styrofoam cup of coffee as the Google home page loaded.

Then he typed in two words: *Maximum Ride*.

37

INSTANTLY, RESULTS POPPED up on the screen—1,704,890 of them in 0.43 seconds. The very first one was an article titled "Winged Children Attend Private School!" Oh, great. Looked like more of that successful "keep a low profile" stuff was going on.

Fang clicked the link and began to read.

As it turned out, the article was a piece from the private school's own online newspaper, the *Newton News*. It spewed out a bunch of glorified info about the flock, accompanied by a hilariously cheesy photo of them posed around the school's marquee, beneath a banner welcoming "Maxine and Co." Fang almost snorted—and then he saw that Dylan had his arm casually thrown around Max.

It was surprising how much that hurt. Especially on

top of the news that Gazzy had blurted out in Paris—that Dylan had been "designed" for Max, and that they were eventually supposed to go out and create little Maxes and Dylans. The concept was still impossible to swallow. Still tasted like crap in his throat.

Fang logged off the computer and dumped his half-finished coffee in the trash. It may have been corny and lame, but the *Newton News* article had given him one thing: the exact location of the flock.

His Voice had told him to go to Max, even though it sure didn't seem like she needed him, all safe in her cushy new digs, with her new boyfriend. Didn't the Voice know how much it hurt Fang to see her? Didn't it know how much he hurt her every time he left?

Maybe it did. Maybe that didn't matter. Maybe something bigger than just the drama of Max and Fang was happening.

At any rate, he knew he had to listen to his Voice.

He had to go back to Max. Whether she wanted him there or not.

38

FANG DIDN'T WANT to admit to the little surge of exhilaration he was feeling at the idea of actually going back to the flock. *Home.* He had tried to put Max out of his head for so long, but for him, "home" would always mean wherever Max was.

It was still barely light. It galled him that he couldn't fly, and instead actually had to hike out to where the main highway passed the town.

He shook his head, thinking of Ari and his cronies. He wouldn't be surprised if the price on his own head was so high that it had infiltrated the backwoods of Middle America, too—Fang knew any driver on the road could be a threat, and it was incredibly stupid for him to hitchhike. But with his painful wing, what choice did he have? He was in the middle of No and Where, and he had no hope of catching a plane or a bus—or even of stealing a car—in this place. He had to get back to Max, so hitching it was.

After an hour and a half spent trudging along with his thumb in the air, Fang's head snapped up at the sound of wheels far down the road. A yellow convertible was speeding down the highway, music blaring.

This time, the car pulled to a slow stop just ahead of him, and he jogged up to it. Three beefy-looking guys peered out of the convertible at him, and Fang felt a twinge of anxiety.

This is stupid, a voice inside him said, and he couldn't tell if it was *the* Voice or just his own rational thought.

"Need a ride?" the driver asked gruffly over the metal music thundering out of the speakers.

Fang glanced down the road. Not a single other car in sight.

"You heading west?" he asked the driver, frowning.

"Yeah."

Fang sighed. The next city was at least twenty miles. It was now or never.

"Then yeah, thanks," he said, hopping into the backseat. Before he'd even sat down, the driver jammed the pedal to the floor. Fang surged backward into the seat, his wing throbbing.

"Hey, watch it!" Fang snapped irritably, but the driver just stared straight ahead with a tight-lipped grin.

The guy in the passenger seat and the guy beside Fang

both stared at him intently, their muscles bulging in their tight T-shirts, their faces twisted into weird expressions.

They looked...hungry. Almost like—Fang's mind balked at the possibility—Erasers?

Or was he just seeing things? It was hard to tell. He didn't trust his own judgment anymore. After Star and Kate's betrayal, everyone seemed suspect.

He stared into the pockmarked face next to him, at the thick neck running up to a crew cut.

No.

They didn't have the right amount of feral wolfishness marring their features to be Erasers. These guys were definitely human. Ugly as all get-out, but human.

So why were they acting so funny? Maybe they were just 'roid heads, Fang thought—crazed on testosterone. He was just being paranoid, that was all.

It's called careful, *you moron,* he imagined Max chiding him. *Always trust your instincts. Paranoia is our way of life.*

But Fang's wing hurt, and he was tired, and at the moment there wasn't a better option than these shady characters. Shady *human* characters, who he could surely take if it came down to it.

Barely five minutes later, the convertible skidded to a stop. "Wow! A scenic overlook!" the driver shouted with over-the-top enthusiasm. "Whattaya say, boys? Should we get a closer look?"

Fang's eyes snapped open. Something was off.

These guys didn't exactly seem like the postcard type.

39

THE THREE GUYS hopped out of the car and strode toward the signs warning pedestrians to keep back from the railing.

"Check out this wicked cliff, fellas," the driver said to his two grinning buddies. They laughed as if he'd just told the most hilarious joke they'd ever heard. "Hey, kid," he called to Fang, "why don't you come over here? I think you'll really wanna see this. You know, up close and personal."

Fang, leaning against the convertible, shook his head. "Nah, I think I'm fine right here, thanks."

He assumed a more defensive position and crossed his arms, but even that small gesture made him wince as his wing bone bent awkwardly. What was *wrong* with him?

The driver grinned. "How's that wing, Fang? Must be giving you some real trouble if you're stooping to hitch-hiking. Really slumming it."

"I'm sorry, do I know you?" Fang asked as casually as possible, but he eyed the trio warily. His instinct had been right. They knew who he was, and they were out to get him. But he could take these guys. If he could fight Erasers, he could definitely handle a few juiced-up punks.

"We're not important, Fang," the driver said soothingly, still looking starved with those hollow eyes. "We're just part of the Plan. But *everybody* knows *you*." He took several steps toward Fang. "You'll be the first, after all."

"Let me guess," Fang said, his dark eyes narrowing. "The first to die."

They charged him then, and relying on instinct rather than thinking, Fang snapped out his wings, his mind calculating rapidly. He'd do a quick up-and-away and jump behind them. He would knock their heads together, leave them sprawled on the asphalt, and beat it out of there.

But that's not what happened at all.

Instead, with that careless wing snap, his injured wing bone ground against itself. Fang groaned in agony and involuntarily hunched over, scrunching his eyes shut as the pain vibrated through him.

And that's all it took.

In the next second they were on him, wrenching his arms backward and digging their elbows into his neck. The driver was violently twisting his hurt wing behind him, and he saw black spots at the same time he felt his knees buckle.

Fang swore through clenched teeth as they started to drag him. He cursed these guys, cursed being alone, cursed the Voice for putting him in this position. This was a perfect storm of crap, all flying through the same fan, right at him.

The three of them worked together to pull Fang to the stone ledge beyond the safety barrier. He felt a singing panic in his veins as he neared the edge of the cliff. This was usually where he would show up to save someone, or someone would show up to save him.

But no one was coming—that was horribly clear. He was more alone than he'd ever been in his life.

The three of them heaved Fang up onto the ledge, kicking and swearing, realizing with growing horror exactly what would happen if he didn't escape *right now*.

He gave another sudden jerk, surging against their grips with all of his strength, and... they let go.

Suddenly, he was free.

Free-*falling*, that is, hurled into empty space, toward the crashing waves of Lake Michigan, broken wing and all. Right off the edge of the cliff.

40

ANGEL SCREAMED FOR what felt like eons, until her own wordless howl hurt her head so much that she shut up. Her throat was raw, her eyes like sandpaper and still unseeing.

She'd had another horribly real nightmare—this time, *Fang* was the one who was dead. She'd seen him falling, falling. . . . Just like she'd seen Maya.

And now Maya was dead.

Angel winced, pressing fingers to her throbbing temples. She lived her own nightmare while she was awake, and she lived others' nightmares when she slept. There was no escape. No escape, ever . . .

Fang.

Angel concentrated, but she couldn't figure out the

ending. She wanted to see, *needed* to see what happened next, even if it was as bad as she feared it was.

But she couldn't.

In her vision, Fang was in a different place than last time. Instead of an empty red desert, the scene had been misty and chilly looking. Instead of the two girls from his gang, there had been three guys there, guys she didn't recognize but instinctively hated. There had been a car. A sunshine-yellow convertible.

And there had been a cliff, dropping sharply and hopelessly down.

Angel felt tears prick her eyes as she relived the last part of the vision. What stuck with her most was the way they'd smiled, those three guys. They'd been beaming like lunatics as they hurled Fang over, leaning over the ledge to watch him fall.

Angel had waited impatiently for Fang to spread his wings and soar away—grinning triumphantly at the evil humans who'd thought they could hurt a *bird kid* by tossing him into the open air. *Ha, ha, morons! Eat my wind!*

But . . . he hadn't.

Hadn't smiled, hadn't taunted them. *Hadn't* spread his wings and soared away.

He'd just dropped, his body twisting and turning awkwardly in the air.

He'd looked broken.

Angel had screamed herself awake from the nightmare right before Fang hit the ground.

But maybe… A tiny part of her whispered, even as she tried to block it out.

Maybe it hadn't been a nightmare after all. Maybe it had been a…vision.

No. No way. She squeezed her eyes shut. "It was a *nightmare*," she said aloud. "It wasn't real."

Like now, she thought. Like the nightmare she was in the middle of living.

Right then a screeching, grating sound filled Angel's ears, like fingernails on a chalkboard.

"Not real, not real," she whispered, even as she shrank back into the shadows of her dog crate.

Moments later, the door to her crate swung open. She pulled herself against the back wall as tightly as she could, ready to come out kicking and punching and screaming.

She expected to feel human hands clenching her, but the sensation was cold, hard, and flat—terrifyingly mechanical. Two large metal paddles had reached in with an awful, gear-grinding sound. They practically filled the crate—there was no way to avoid them. Angel ducked high and low, but eventually the paddles closed in on her, clamping onto her body firmly, leaving her no room to writhe or wiggle free.

With more metallic grinding, the paddles began to retreat, dragging Angel out of the dog crate roughly. Then she found herself suspended in midair, held up by what must have been two warehouse cargo-moving forceps. She shouted and twisted this way and that as she moved through empty air. Then she was dumped unceremoniously on a hard surface. She felt the crisp sheets crinkle against her legs and almost wept with defeat.

An operating table.

Again.

She was too exhausted to struggle. What was the point? They would find a way to make her cooperate. She had no more tears left, so she lay dry-eyed as her arms and legs were clamped to the sides of the table.

"This is for your own good," someone told her—a whitecoat whose voice she didn't recognize. "We need to make sure there's no way you can escape these tests."

Angel's heart clenched. More tests. What could they possibly do now? Hadn't they already taken samples of skin, bone, blood, and feathers? How could they not know every square inch of her, down to the cellular level?

Another pair of cold metal forceps moved along her shoulder blades. They reached under her back, then forcibly unfurled her wings, pulling them out from beneath her. Her wings, too, were clamped to the operating table.

She tried to fight the nausea, but felt bile rising in her throat.

They'd never done this before. Never.

A whole new level of fear streaked through Angel's body. She realized what was coming right before it actually happened.

Small snipping noises filtered into her brain, followed by a pinching sensation at her primary feathers.

"Done," the whitecoat said. "Good little mutant." He left the lab, his footsteps fading away as the door closed, leaving Angel clamped to the operating table. She remained silent the entire time, mute with shock and horror.

They'd clipped her wings.

41

EVERYTHING IS ABOUT to change, the Voice said. *Prepare yourselves.*

Every single member of the flock heard it.

Your task is to record what happens.

Nudge yelped and dropped the bottle of glue, leaving a glittery blue stain on her scrapbook.

"What—" she began, but was interrupted by the Voice.

Write, blog, take videos on a cell phone—it doesn't matter. Just make sure you record everything, down to the last detail. Everything. You have to record it all—for the future.

A Voice in her head. Another huge clue that she was a freak. Nudge wanted to cry, wanted to scream at the Voice to leave her alone, to let her at least pretend to be kind of normal! Nudge clenched her jaw and determinedly went back to making her scrapbook of normal, wingless girls.

Nudge, this is about the future. In the future, you will be normal. In the future, you might even get sick of feeling average. But right now, the world needs you. The Voice sounded unusually gentle. *This task is the most important thing you will ever do for humankind. So get up, grab your phone, and start keeping a log—for the future.*

Nudge hesitated. This felt really urgent. She didn't want any part of this. But she knew one thing: Max never went against the Voice. Nudge sighed, her shoulders slumping. There would be no normalcy today. "Okay," Nudge said, defeated. "Okay."

Don't let Max out of your sight.

Iggy and the Gasman, in separate rooms, both sat up, listening. The Voice. They'd heard it only once or twice before. They were hearing it now. Like before, it seemed important, vital, that they do what it said.

You must protect Max at any cost—even your own lives, the Voice said. *She must survive to lead. The calm is over. The storm is on the way, and the skies will break open with its force. Do you understand?*

Not really, Gazzy thought, peering outside at the blameless blue sky. No menacing dark clouds, no swarms of locusts, no angry mobs. But he knew the Voice was right about one thing—he needed Max as a leader, and if her life was in danger, he was absolutely willing to protect her from weather or whitecoats or whatever else came along.

Gazzy stood up, ready to go find her, then hesitated. *Don't let Max out of your sight.* Did the Voice really mean never *ever* let her out of his sight, no matter what? Surely Max would need bathroom breaks? What had the Voice said? Protect her with his own life! Well, of course, and that sounded like they would definitely need explosives before too long. But...

In the kitchen, Iggy was holding a mixer blade as cake batter dripped, unnoticed, onto his shirt. He had to protect Max? Even at the cost of his own life? He cocked his head, listening intently. He could hear nothing out of the ordinary—no vehicles or choppers on their way, no one shouting alarms. Total wasn't even barking, not that he usually did. But for some reason the Voice needed his help. Right in the middle of this cake.

"Okay. She'll survive without my help—she's too stubborn to die," Iggy muttered. "But I'll protect her anyway."
Good.

Harden your heart.

Why, hello there, Voice, I thought snidely. *It's nice to see you, too. How's tricks?*

There's no time for jokes, Maximum. Time has run out. The end is here, Max. Now.

I stopped slashing wing holes in the back of a hoodie

and frowned. *The end? Like the apocalypse? No offense, but if I had a nickel for every time I'd heard that—*

This is no time to be getting soft, to let your guard down, Max. You're not as paranoid as you used to be. You're not as strong.

Hey, I am just *as paranoid as I ever was,* I thought defensively. *Our life here just happens to be on the calm and peaceful side of the spectrum. For once.*

Listen very closely, Max. Your task, at the end, is to harden your heart.

Harden my heart? Like, further? Isn't that what everyone has always complained about with me? Now it's a good thing?

Lives will be lost. More than you can imagine. In order to survive, you must harden yourself against their suffering. Lose the softness. Become the fearless leader again.

I scowled at the implication that I'd ever been less than a "fearless leader," but I had to admit, I was rattled—as much by the Voice, whose word I'd always taken as gospel, saying that the end was finally here as by the Voice, who had told me I had to save the world in the first place, telling me to put myself first. My mind recoiled at the confusion, and at the Voice's hardness.

Its certainty.

I waited for the Voice to say something else, but it was silent—apparently my brain was only mine again. As messed up as that sounds.

Dread gnawing at my insides, I pondered my task: to harden my heart. Come what may.

42

EVERYTHING IS ABOUT to change. Dylan paused the video game he was playing. He looked around, but no one was near him. *Prepare yourselves.* Was this his... Voice? He knew Max, and possibly the other members of the flock, had heard it before, but this was totally new to him.

Um... what do you want? he thought. For a second, he was almost excited. It was like he was one of them—even more like Max—now that he had a Voice, too.

But his excitement quickly went cold.

You have a task ahead of you, Dylan. One that only you can perform. One that you must perform. Do you understand?

This sounded familiar. Dylan fought a wave of nausea as he remembered Dr. Williams describing the other task he had to perform—bringing Fang in for a life of torture.

Now this weird Voice in his head was demanding something else of him that he supposedly couldn't refuse....

What is it? Dylan thought with dread.

The answer wasn't anything he would have predicted.

You must fully win Max's heart. The survival of the world depends on it.

Dylan groaned and dropped his head into his hands. "Like I haven't been trying!" he said aloud, exasperated. *Is that all? Sure you don't have any dragons I can slay instead?*

A nice, solid, physical goal. That was what he needed. He was pretty confident about his physical abilities—flying skills, fighting technique, speed, strength.

But Max's heart... Max was an enigma wrapped in a puzzle wrapped in a cipher. Or something. He'd been trying to win her over ever since he'd joined the flock. Every once in a while, it felt like he was making headway. Dylan's face flushed as he remembered the few mind-blowing kisses they'd shared.

But then she would back off again, and he would be left wondering what he'd done wrong, and if he would ever, *ever* get it right.

Now the Voice, the not-to-be-ignored Voice, was saying he had to somehow step up his game and actually win Max's heart. For the sake of the entire world. Dylan felt panicky. It wasn't like winning Max's heart was taking one for the team. It was the only thing he'd ever wanted.

But until now, he'd never been afraid of what would happen if he failed.

43

GOING ON A dream date is not exactly "hardening your heart," Max, I thought to myself uneasily, remembering the Voice's creepy warning. If being closed off were an Olympic sport, I'd have more gold medals than I could carry. But this whole heart-hardening gig simply was not happening.

Not now. Not tonight.

Because, despite my usual reaction to all things girly (eye roll, look of disgust, general feeling of nausea), tonight I was positively giddy and swooning. I couldn't help it—I had seriously underestimated the effect a little romance can have on a girl.

Dream date.

Unlike the general population, my idea of a dream date would once have been simply defined as not eating roasted lizard or Dumpster scraps for dinner. But my first (second? Did the one at the movies count?) "date" with Dylan was certainly more than that.

Much, much more, in fact.

I stared up at the sight before me, jaw on the ground and eyes bugging. See, when Dylan came up to me after school and said "Follow me," I thought, *What the heck? I'll just go ahead and follow the guy, let him show me whatever fascinating new discovery he's made.* I had expected him to demonstrate that he could fly backward or show me a cool rock formation he'd found—something like that.

Let me tell you: I was not expecting *this*.

"H-how did you...?" I stuttered. We were nestled within the branches of a huge fir tree, about thirty feet up. I felt the warmth of Dylan's hand on my lower back, steadying me as I leaned backward and gaped up, still trying to take in all the amazing details of the house. *My* house.

"I've been building it ever since we got here," Dylan said, smiling shyly at my speechless astonishment. "I went exploring the first day and found this tree, and I knew you liked tree houses...."

I grinned dopily at his perfect face, his soft, anxious eyes. *I knew you liked tree houses.* Dylan had taken the time to listen to what I liked, had been making notes about things that made me happy. The guy had actually been *paying attention*.

And this... this was more than a tree house. It was like the Swiss Family Robinson tree house, Oregon edition. It had a floor, walls, windows, a roof. All of it was beautifully constructed out of branches and planks, and sort of camouflaged with leafy twigs and vines. From the ground, it would blend with the rest of the tree canopy. But from up here, on this branch, it was stunning. I saw a doorway covered with a green cloth curtain.

"Come on," Dylan said, taking my hand.

Together we leaped the fifteen feet from the branch to the balcony that ran around three sides of the tree house. Dylan held open the door curtain and the warm glow of candlelight flowed out into the deepening dusk. That's right—candlelight. The whole shebang.

I swallowed and stepped inside. When Dylan dropped the curtain, it shut out the rest of the world. Dylan and I were alone, out here in the mountain woods, a five-minute flight away from Newton and the rest of the flock.

Dylan looked at my face intently, as if trying to read my expression. I felt the flush creeping up my cheeks, my heart getting all loud and poundy. The combination of the violet dusk and the yellow candlelight made his features even more unbelievably gorgeous.

I turned away from him and walked around the space, running my fingers over the gleaming wood, seeing the notched joints, the clever design. It wasn't huge inside—maybe eight feet by eight feet. But it was cozy, and plenty big enough. *For what?* I wondered.

"I stole the supplies from woodworking class," Dylan said, answering my unasked question. "Do you like it?"

"I *love* it," I murmured, with more ache in my voice than I'd intended. "It's so th—"

I stopped and sniffed the air.

"So th...? *So th* what?"

"Do I smell...food?"

"You do indeed," said Dylan. "Roast chicken, pasta, buttery garlic bread, and—"

"*Chocolate cake?*" I moaned. There was a short, square table in the middle of the room, set up with two pillows to sit on. To the left was a low shelf holding everything my hypersensitive-when-it-comes-to-sniffing-out-all-edible-things nose had caught, plus more.

Dylan's face lit up with another grin, and he made a sweeping gesture for me to sit on one of the pillows. I sank down, starting to wonder if this was just an elaborate dream my traitorous subconscious had concocted. No one had ever done anything like this for me before. No one had ever gone to so much trouble for me. It was...unnerving. I looked up at Dylan and felt—what?

Gratitude. Gratitude and pure happiness. Right there, in that moment, *he* seemed too amazing to be real.

Dylan sat down on the other side of the table and passed me a plate—a *real* plate, not, like, a paper one—and a glass of sparkling cider. It was so prim and proper I almost—*almost*—wished I was wearing a dress or something.

"Eat dinner with me?" Dylan asked shyly. I could feel the heat of the candle between us as the reflection of its flame flickered gorgeously in his eyes.

"Heck yeah," I said as normally as possible, ignoring the fact that my heart was rumbling even more than my stomach. "Pass the chicken."

We spent the next few minutes in silence as we worked our way through the delicious dishes in a way that only calorie-starved mutants avoiding sticky emotions and heightened sexual tension could. I was on my last bite of my third piece of chocolate cake when Dylan leaned toward the window and stuck his head out into the night. He whistled, low and long, like a Native American signal or something.

Wha? I thought.

And then Iggy appeared in the doorway, carrying a silver platter and—get this—wearing a bow tie. I kid you not. Okay, the bow tie was worn over a ratty, laundry-deficient T-shirt, but still.

"Iggy?" I said, stating the obvious. I shifted awkwardly, eyeing the candlelight and suddenly relieved that I was still in my plain old jeans after all. I imagined the flock gathering later, singing "Maaax has a boyyy-friiiiend" in chorus. I guess our date wasn't as private as I'd thought. I didn't know how I felt about that.

"Thanks, man," Dylan said, striding over and taking the platter. "You know you weren't required to wear a bow tie...."

"Sometimes a man just has to suit up," Iggy replied. He crossed his pale arms and puffed out his chest proudly. "This was one of those times."

"And I appreciate it." Dylan nodded, obscuring the

mysterious new platter from my sight. "Thanks again. You remember the next part of the mission?"

"Mission Entertain Gazzy and Nudge So They Don't Get Bored and Cause Major Property Damage or Worse is well under way. You and Max are good to go, dude."

"Good to go where?" I demanded, but Iggy just wiggled his eyebrows at me.

With one last salute and a tweak of his bow tie, which he had gotten from God knows where, Iggy ducked through the door curtain and flew off into the dark night. Dylan came back to sit across the table from me. He set the platter between us and took off the lid, revealing neat piles of graham crackers, chocolate bars, and marshmallows.

"I've always wanted to try to make s'mores with a candle. Shall we?"

"You've thought of everything, haven't you?" I said, simultaneously reaching for a marshmallow and popping a graham cracker in my mouth.

"Well, I tried." Dylan smiled. Then his expression grew slightly more serious. "I swear I'll win your heart in the end, Max."

I coughed out graham cracker crumbs. My cheeks flushed and I tucked a piece of hair behind my ear. Suddenly I felt squirmy and smoldering and turbulent inside, like a million hot coals had been poured into my stomach.

But to be honest, it wasn't such a bad feeling.

44

"I DON'T THINK the candle-marshmallow thing is working," I said. "I've been holding mine over the flame for, like, a billion years now, and it's barely browning."

The air was soft and cool and smelled like rosemary and pine sap and smoke from the candles. Outside the tree house, it was a pitch-black night. Inside it was all cozy, golden light, flickering shadows on the walls. I practically had to stop myself from hyperventilating from the sheer *romance* of it all.

"We might be forced to eat raw s'mores," Dylan agreed solemnly, but I saw the crinkles at the corners of his eyes when he looked at me.

That was when I realized just how close we were sitting.

"You know, some people really like raw s'mores," I mumbled, licking my lips.

And then, before I could talk myself out of it, I dropped my marshmallow on the table, leaned forward, and kissed Dylan.

Right on the mouth. On purpose. Yes. You read it here first.

For a second he was startled, but then he responded, bringing his hands up to cup my face. His lips moved against mine slowly, gently, softly. It was a quiet kiss. A tentative kiss. An innocent, feathery, earth-shatteringly *right* kiss.

And I wanted more.

I edged closer to him and wrapped my arms around his neck, tangling my fingers in his dark blond hair. I tasted the chocolate from the s'mores on his tongue, and our mouths moved together almost like a duel, a graceful and elegant kata—

"Aaagh! My eyes!"

Dylan and I froze for an instant, and then sprang apart as if electrified.

"That was Nudge's surprised squawk," I said. My voice was hoarse and I cleared my throat, my mind reeling over what I'd just been doing, what I'd just been feeling. My face was hot, my hands were trembling, and my lips were all tingly.

"Nudge? Is something wrong?" Dylan said, instantly on the alert.

Slowly Nudge's face edged around the green cloth curtain.

"Um, sorry." She coughed, looking at me in fascination. "Nothing's wrong. I was just surprised. 'Cause I, uh, fell. Off a branch. Er...pretend I was never here."

I stood up, mortified, but also angry. It had been hard enough to take the leap to kiss Dylan without having the entire world know about it. "Were you spying on me? On us?" I asked, narrowing my eyes.

"I'm not the only one!" she protested sheepishly. "It's not what you think! Look, hold on." Nudge ducked outside for a moment and called out, "Gazzy! Ig! Get in here— the jig is up!"

"'The jig is up'?" I repeated. "Gazzy? Iggy?" Dylan came to stand next to me, his hand warm on my back. I suppressed the memory of what we had been doing a minute earlier, and crossed my arms over my chest.

"Way to be a traitor, Nudge," I heard Gazzy say. Then both he and Iggy (who was still wearing his bow tie) entered the tree house behind Nudge.

The three of them stood there, fidgeting and looking anywhere but at me and Dylan.

I went for the classic interrogation technique: Hit the weakest link first. Nudge had never been good at lying to me. "Nudge," I said, pointing, "explain what's going on. I thought you guys were at home. *Obviously.*"

She squirmed.

"*Nudge,*" I pressed. Leader Max was back in business. Romancey Max had been squashed for the time being.

"Um," she said, moving her hands out from behind her

back. She was holding some sort of box-type thing, silver and black. . . .

A video camera. A freaking video camera.

I gaped. I felt like my face had spontaneously burst into flames at the same time as my legs had melted into a puddle. "Were you *filming* us?"

Nudge nodded uncomfortably.

I strode forward to plant myself right in front of the three conniving little thugs, nearly hissing in rage. "Why on *earth* would you *film* that?"

"YouTube?" Iggy suggested totally unhelpfully, and I had to actually mentally count to ten to restrain myself.

"I'm s'posed to record everything," Nudge mumbled.

"What? Why? What are you *talking* about?"

She didn't answer. I rounded on Iggy and the Gasman. "And you! What were you two doing?"

"Sitting in the trees outside," Gazzy replied in a small voice. Good to know I hadn't completely lost my touch. "Making sure."

"Making. Sure. Of. What."

"Um . . . that you were safe?" he squeaked.

I made a half-shrieking, half-choking sound. "Since when can I not take care of myself? I was with Dylan, for Pete's sake! We were"—I faltered slightly but kept on truckin'—"eating dinner! What were you three *thinking*?"

They all remained silent.

"I can't *believe* you," I spat. "Give me the video camera, Nudge."

Nudge didn't move.

"Nudge. Camera. *Now*."

"I can't!" she cried, putting it behind her back again. "It's my job! I have to!"

That was when I really lost it. I snarled and, without thinking, shot out my foot in a sideways kick. Luckily, I didn't kick Dylan, Iggy, Gazzy, or Nudge. Unluckily, I kicked the table.

Which had candles on it.

It all happened before I could even blink.

The tall tapers fell sideways, and hot wax ran across the table and onto the floor.

Instantly the wax ignited, sending trails of flame through the tree house.

The fire zipped along seams in the wood at lightning speed.

Then it sparked at the spiky needles of the fir tree, which were poking in through one of the windows, and in the next instant the dried twigs and vines overhead caught.

"*Crap*," I said in miserable awe, as suddenly we were caught in a living torch, the tree going up in flames all around us. Well, let's just assume I said "crap."

"Everybody out!" Dylan shouted, and the five of us jumped through the doorway, one after another, unfurling our wings and flapping until we were all hovering in the cold mountain air above the forest.

I looked at Dylan and felt utterly helpless as we both watched his beautiful creation go up in flames—the tree house he'd spent who knows how many hours to make, just for me.

A perfect gift for a perfect evening, and I'd destroyed it.

"I'm so sorry, Dylan," I whispered miserably, my voice breaking. "It was beautiful. I didn't mean to. It was the most beautiful thing I've ever seen."

He gave a little smile at that, the rise and fall of his wings in perfect timing with mine. "No," he said softly. "You're the most beautiful thing I've ever seen."

My heart surged and I started to smile, but just then the tree gave a terrific crack, as the fire hissed its way through the wood. And as I watched the thick plume of smoke billowing upward, I heard the echo of the Voice's words in my head, and I couldn't shake the icy feeling that the burning tree was some sort of horrible omen.

45

YOU'D THINK THAT would be enough excitement for one evening—the pinnacle of romance in my life, my unintended destruction of same—but no. I was awakened in the middle of the night by wailing alarms that made me bolt upright in my bed.

Don't ask me how Iggy and the Gasman got the supplies to make the alarms, or when they rigged the entire house; I've been asking myself those same dang questions our whole lives together, and I still don't know the answers. I jumped out of bed, wide-eyed and ready to rumble.

Out in the hall, Gazzy stumbled out of his bedroom. "Whuzzappenin'?" he mumbled. His blond hair was scruffy with bedhead. "We under attack?" He stifled a huge yawn.

"I don't know. Maybe," I replied tightly. "Head count!

Iggy? Nudge? Total? And Dylan?" *Note to self: Stop blushing at any mention of Dylan. Total giveaway.*

"Yeah, yeah," Iggy said irritably, making his way to us with unerring accuracy. Nudge was behind him, rubbing sleep out of her eyes. Iggy pulled a small black remote from the pocket of his sweatpants and clicked a button. The alarms instantly went silent.

Dylan arrived just then, looking like a freaking pajama model. We glanced at each other briefly before I chickened out and looked away. You know your life is sad when possibly being under attack is more appealing than facing the guy you made out with just a few hours earlier.

Thankfully, that was when Total showed up to make the little midnight powwow complete, so I had a good distraction.

"I was right in the middle of a dream about my lovely lady," Total growled, flopping down on the floor with his head on his paws. "This better be good. Is it the whitecoats? Erasers? Flyboys? Mr. Chu monster things? Land sharks? Mini-Godzillas?"

I rolled my eyes. "Don't know. Iggy, where were the alarms set up? What were they rigged for?"

"They're around the perimeter," Iggy said, shrugging. "Nothing small would set them off, like a squirrel. It's something big."

Nudge dropped down and crawled to a window, where she rose a tiny bit and peered out, squinting. "It's too dark. I can't see anything."

"Okay, everyone—get ready for whatever it is," I said grimly. "Let's wait thirty seconds, and then we'll hit the sky to do recon."

"Fine," said Iggy. "I'll get some firearms." He headed down the hall.

At the window, Nudge frowned and squinted harder, cupping her hands around her eyes to get a better view of the darkness outside.

I dropped and crawled over to her. "See something?"

"Yeah," she murmured. "Seven o'clock." She pointed carefully. "See that shadow? I think someone's out there, walking toward the house."

"Who is it?" Gazzy asked, also dropping down. "Is it Jeb?"

"No, it's—" Nudge's breath hitched in her throat. "That doesn't make sense. Oh, my gosh. *It couldn't be.*"

"What?" I asked, already mentally preparing a defense, an attack, a plan to escape. I pressed my face against the cool glass of the window, but even with my raptor vision, I couldn't pinpoint what Nudge was seeing. "Couldn't be *what*? Or *who*?"

Nudge drew back and faced us, looking utterly shocked. "It's *Fang.*"

46

THE WIND HAD been knocked out of me as surely as if Nudge had socked me in the gut.

"Fang?" I asked weakly, peering out the window again. "What do you mean, *Fang*? It can't be. He's walking." The strangled sound of my voice vibrated in my ears.

"I saw his face when he passed through a beam of moonlight," answered Nudge. "It's either Fang or a perfect clone."

A clone. Yeah, that was it. A clone like Ari, sent as a decoy by some whitecoat trying to sabotage us. *It can't be the real Fang*, I told myself—Fang was *gone*. I let my breath out, relieved at the idea of fighting some potential threat rather than dealing with the possibilities of what Fang's return would mean.

"Why is he limping?" Gazzy asked, squinting through the blinds.

"He's *limping*?" I remained still for a split second longer, then rose and practically threw myself down the hallway with the flock on my heels.

Gazzy flung open the front door and flicked on the porch light. I sucked in my breath, and my heart nearly exploded.

The figure that blinked up at us from ten yards away was absolutely, unmistakably Fang.

I gasped at the state he was in. He looked as if he could barely stand. His face was grayish and drawn, his shoulders hunched. His clothes were filthy. One arm hung uselessly by his side, and one wing was caked with dried blood. He looked like the living dead.

"*Fang!*" Nudge shrieked, and, ignoring all the rules I'd taught her about the million possibilities of danger, bounded off the porch in a blur of pink nightgown. She reached him in one leap, ignoring his obvious injuries and jumping into his arms.

I stepped out onto the porch, scanning the area for threats, but there was obviously no point. It was the real Fang, all right. Nothing else could explain why I felt so tingly and weird all over.

The hairs on the back of my neck prickled, and I realized Dylan was standing right behind me. His fingers reached out to hold me at my waist, and I tried to subtly move away. But subtlety has never been my strong suit, and Dylan sighed loudly.

"Fang!" Iggy whooped. He and the Gasman followed Nudge off the porch, and the three guys exchanged those weird half-hug frat-boy things where they pat one another on the back. Even Total ran forward, putting his front paws against Fang's leg, wagging his tail.

"Go on," Dylan told me. "You know you want to." His voice was bitter, so different from the gentle tone he'd used in the tree house. I could hear the implication in that tone and resented it, even as I felt myself moving from the doorway.

Fang detached himself from Nudge and looked up. Our eyes met, and just like that, my legs hurtled me forward and suddenly I was hugging him tightly. Fang's uninjured arm went around my shoulders.

"You came back," I whispered, hating the longing in my voice.

"Did you think I wouldn't?" he asked with a half smile that was infuriating and devastating and revealed nothing and everything at the same time.

A smile I had known all my life.

Fang felt...familiar. Warm—as warm as Dylan had felt, just a few short hours earlier in the tree house.

As I buried my face in Fang's dirty, bloodied hair, I felt Dylan's eyes boring into my back, and tried to swallow my guilt.

47

FOOD HAS ALWAYS been our number one solution for any awkward situation, so Iggy had the bright idea of whipping up a Welcome Back cake for Fang. This was undoubtedly to save us from the semi-uncomfortable silence that followed once I finally managed to peel myself from Fang's grimy, sweaty body.

It may shock you to learn that Dylan decided to skip Fang's Welcome Back party. Said he had homework. But I could *feel* his glowering energy radiating through the house while the rest of us were making fake conversation in the kitchen, pretending that the newest member of the flock didn't exist.

I avoided trying to figure out the who, what, where, when, how, and *why* of Fang's return by forcing Iggy to let *me* bake the cake—maybe a first—and then serving it up. Almost without thinking, I scraped the icing off Fang's slice of cake before I put it in front of him (he'd never been a fan of icing) and plopped a quart of chocolate milk down for him to chug out of the carton, like he always used to do. Like he was still a little kid.

He looked up at me with a dull smirk. "Been taking home ec?"

My face turned red. Was he disgusted, like I didn't know him anymore? Or did he think it was sweet, like I'd *always* known him, and always would?

I'd been pacing around the kitchen, avoiding eye contact with him, for forty-five minutes. Now I finally planted myself across the table from him and stared intently at his beaten face. His hair had grown shaggy and long, and he'd aged several years in a matter of months.

He'd become a man.

At first the thought made me a little sad. And then it kind of scared me. But then it actually...*excited* me, somehow.

And what have you become, Maximum Ride? I thought. Definitely *not* a woman. And definitely not a savior. Barely a leader, anymore. Basically, I was nothing.

"So...no offense, man, but why're you here?" Iggy asked, his mouth fully loaded with cake, spraying us all with chocolate crumbs. "Shouldn't you be with your gang?"

Fang shoved a hunk of cake into his mouth. He glanced at Iggy and shrugged. Fang was giving us the silent treatment, just like old times.

"I'm just looking for some answers, man," pressed Iggy.

"The gang is done," Fang answered shortly, taking a swig of the chocolate milk. A shadow passed over his face, and I remembered what Ari had said about Maya. "So, how's Dylan doing?"

Dylan, the elephant in the room (well, in the living room). The rest of the flock stared at me expectantly. Iggy whistled, and Gazzy made kissing noises.

"Out!" I yelled at them. They scrambled away, taking the rest of the cake with them.

"Dylan's fine," I told him, as nonchalantly as possible. "Doing well on his flying and fighting techniques, adjusting in the community, you know..."

"Uh-huh." Fang stared at me, his dark eyes focusing on me intently, a tight little smile on his lips. "You look... different, Max. Lighter, or happier, or something."

Or something.

"Is that supposed to be a compliment?" I snorted dismissively, but inside, my stomach leaped a little. Was he trying to say I looked *good*? Maybe even... *pretty*?

"I guess Dylan was just what the doctor ordered," Fang went on, unlocking his eyes from mine abruptly and stabbing his fork into his cake.

"Yeah, right. The insane Dr. Gunther-Hagen, that is. I really trust the guy." I coughed. "Anyway, thanks, but... you actually look a little like roadkill, and I'm pretty freaking worried. What *happened*?"

He gave me a penetrating stare that made me shiver—

not unpleasantly—from my neck to my toes. "Basically, I came back from the dead, Max. And I'm ready to move on now. End of story."

As if it wasn't bad enough that my evening with Dylan in the tree house had pretty much filled my every thought up until about an hour ago, now that Fang was back I was having flashbacks of kisses with *him*.

The different memories kept swirling through my head like a swarm of tadpoles in a muddy pond, twisting into darker and darker masses of shapes until I couldn't tell which way was up.

Or which intensely beautiful winged boy I was fantasizing about.

48

FANG AND DYLAN stood across from each other, both silent, arms crossed. Dylan shifted his weight, rubbed absently at his temple. It wasn't like he was facing the mostly-ex-but-it-was-confusing boyfriend of the girl he loved or anything.

"You wanted to talk to me about something?" Dylan asked finally, cursing the anxiety he heard in his own voice and envying the expression on Fang's face—that cool blankness that gave nothing away.

"Yeah," Fang replied quietly, yet with so much hostility in the single word that Dylan was taken by surprise.

The time away from the flock had left Fang leaner, more angular. Add in the amount of still healing bruises and cuts on his face and the pissed-off scowl, and Fang looked downright menacing.

Not that Dylan couldn't take him in a fight, if it came to that. He totally could. But still. An ideal situation, this wasn't.

"So . . . ?" Dylan said after another long minute of uncomfortable silence. "Talk."

"I heard you've been sleeping in Max's room," Fang said, his dark eyes narrowing.

Ohhhh. So that's what this is about, Dylan thought. *Note to self: There is a reason Max calls Nudge "the Vortex of Friendly, Chattery, Bambi-Eyed Doom." She sees, hears, and talks about all.*

"Yeah, and?" Dylan said, feigning as much boredom as he could muster. He even picked at his fingernails.

"And"—Fang leaned forward—"that's not necessary."

Dylan put up his hands. "Look, you don't need to get all alpha on me, man." Regardless of his history with Fang, he wasn't about to actually fight him there, in the middle of the house. Especially not after all the headway he'd made with Max. "I just like to sleep there. There's nothing going on," Dylan said, and instantly wished he hadn't.

"Oh, nothing's going on?" Fang barked out a laugh that made Dylan flush with humiliation. "No kidding, Casanova. You don't need to tell me that much—Max has standards, after all."

Dylan opened his mouth to protest, to tell this jerk

exactly what kind of standards Max had, to blurt out every detail about the scene in the tree house—Max's mouth, Max's skin, Max's soft feathers under his hands. But in that instant Dylan also saw what would follow—the hurt on Max's face, the accusation—and stopped short.

"Look, maybe you think you're protecting her or something," Fang continued. "Who knows? But she's safe here, with all of us around her. She doesn't need you curled up at the foot of her bed like a lovesick dog."

Dylan clamped his lips shut and tried to talk himself out of decking Fang. *Not worth it*, he told himself.

"So you can stop *protecting* her," Fang said. "I'm back now. The flock is together again." He faltered for a split second, and Dylan knew exactly which person had just crossed his mind—a small blond person with white wings. "Max is fine."

Now it was Dylan's turn to laugh. He looked at Fang coolly. "Excuse me? You're back now, so automatically everything's good again? Who do you think you're kidding? Things got worse the moment you came crawling back through that door."

"What's that supposed to mean?" demanded Fang. "Worse for you, you mean, now that your little dream world is ending?"

Dylan ignored that. "You're supposedly doing this all for Max, right?" he challenged. Fang nodded, leaning back against the doorjamb. "Well, sorry to break it to you, but by coming back, all you've done is put Max in more danger." Dylan sighed and sat on the edge of his bed, resting his elbows on his knees.

Silence. Then: "What?"

Dylan looked at Fang with a level gaze. "Haven't you noticed that, like, the entire world is hunting you?" he asked.

Fang shifted. "They're after all of us. They always have been," Fang said quietly, but he was frowning.

"You seriously don't know? You're the one they want, not *Max*, not the rest of the flock!" Dylan was shouting now. "It's *you*, Fang. It's your DNA they're after."

"You're joking."

"I'm not."

"*My* DNA?" Fang laughed, but it sounded tinny and hollow to Dylan's ears. "My DNA is, like, Generation *Zero*."

"Well, fifty-fourth, actually," Dylan said. "But apparently they discovered something that has every whitecoat in the world after you."

"Who did? I don't believe you," Fang spat, but the uncertainty in his eyes—the fear—betrayed him. "What kind of discovery could they possibly make about me that I wouldn't know?"

Dylan let out a breath. "I . . . can't tell you."

Fang pushed off the doorjamb and crossed the bedroom in two strides. He stood in front of Dylan, fists clenched, the veins in his neck straining. "You can't tell me? And why is that? Because you're making this up? Because a little bird told you? Because you're on their side?"

"I'm on the side of Max surviving," Dylan shot back. "I didn't make this up. But I can't tell you the details unless—"

"Unless what?" Fang's voice was tight.

"Unless you swear to leave . . . and never come back."

They stared at each other, black eyes locked onto blue, night and day.

"I can't swear that," Fang said in a low voice.

Dylan's jaw clenched. "Then I can't be held accountable for anything I do to you. You're putting her in danger. You're putting everyone in danger. Don't you even care?"

"My Voice said to be with Max," answered Fang. "I'm never leaving her again."

49

"PAWS OFF, BUCKO," I barked, slapping the Gasman's hands away from my slice of pie. "You already ate an entire half of the pie. Your pie privileges have been revoked."

"Paws off?" Total said, looking up from his plate. "I resent that. You're saying that all pie stealers have paws? Is that it?"

"Chillax," I told Total. I'd forgotten he was sitting there. "It's just a turn of phrase."

"Hmph," said Total.

"And you," I said, turning back to Gazzy. "Step. Away. From. The. Pie."

"Poop," Gazzy mumbled. "Dylan wouldn't give me any of his, either. Neither would Nudge. Or Iggy."

"And what have we learned from this experience?" I asked, raising one eyebrow.

Gazzy shuffled. "Um…everyone but me needs to work on their sharing skills?"

"No," I said patiently. "We learned that if you eat half a pie, you get your pie privileges taken away. Capiche?"

I am such a good not-mom.

The Gasman started to say something else but was cut off by the sudden appearance of Fang, who had entered the living room like a freaking shadow.

Just like old times.

I glanced at Fang and was startled by how pale he was. His normally inexpressive face looked taut, and his lips were pressed into a thin white line.

"What's wrong?" I said immediately, getting ready to do a head count. "Is everyone okay?"

Fang hesitated. "Can you come with me?"

I took one last bite of pie, then followed Fang down the hallway, past Nudge's room, Iggy's room, Gazzy's, mine, Dylan's, and Total's. (Yes, the dog got his own room.)

Fang opened the door to the guest room and led me inside. His laptop was open and running on the bed, and I saw the page for his blog pulled up on the screen.

"Wait, this is about your *blog*?" I exclaimed, one part relieved and two parts annoyed that he'd gotten me all worked up for nothing. "From your face, I thought we were gearing up for Armageddon!"

He sat and motioned to the laptop. "Read the comment on top."

Great. Probably another Fang fan-girl (Fang-irl?) gushing about how incredibly *guh-orrrrr-geous* he was. I sighed and sat down next to him on the bed.

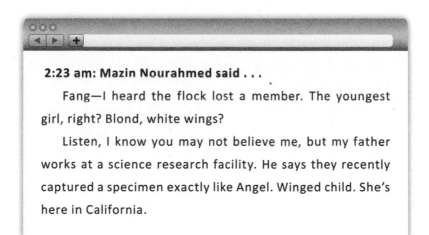

2:23 am: Mazin Nourahmed said . . .

Fang—I heard the flock lost a member. The youngest girl, right? Blond, white wings?

Listen, I know you may not believe me, but my father works at a science research facility. He says they recently captured a specimen exactly like Angel. Winged child. She's here in California.

What? My heart stopped. I couldn't breathe.

Feeling completely numb—I refused to get my hopes up—I clicked on the image that came with the comment. Fang and I were both silent, waiting with bated breath, as the image loaded.

It was a blurry, grainy photo, maybe taken on an old cell phone. The background was dark and murky, with a couple of blocky shadows that looked a bit like hospital equipment. I ignored that and focused on the foreground, which had better lighting.

Better lighting that revealed a chunk of limp blond

ringlets. A clump of dirty white feathers. A small, pale hand—the same hand I'd held a million times throughout the years.

"Oh, my God," I breathed. "Oh, my God."

Fang leaned toward the computer screen, gazing at the photo. "So you think it's really her?" he asked softly. I caught the faint undercurrents of insane, wild, un-Fang-like excitement.

"Yeah," I squeaked, hardly believing I was saying it. "Yes," I said louder, looking into his eyes and seeing my own certainty reflected there. "Fang, I think that's Angel."

"*What?*"

It wasn't Fang who'd spoken. The two of us turned to the doorway to see Nudge and Gazzy staring at us. Gazzy was holding the second pie, and Nudge was carrying two forks. Under different circumstances, I'd have whooped their conniving, thieving little behinds. But right now, all I could do was frantically process plans, ideas, possibilities, while I tried to contain the enormous hopeful smile that was threatening to take over my face.

"Angel," said Fang. "Angel might be alive."

The Gasman gasped and dropped the pie, which splattered all over the floor. None of us even flinched. "*What?*" he said again.

"Look," I choked out, and he and Nudge hurried over to the bed. I watched as they read this Mazin Nourahmed person's comment and studied the photo.

"Trap?" Nudge asked immediately. *That's my girl.*

"Maybe," I replied. Then I regretfully added: "Probably."

"Do we care?" That was Gazzy. I knew how much he wanted to see his little sister again—under any circumstances.

Fang and I glanced at each other, then answered at the same time: "No."

The four of us sat there for a few more moments, just letting the news sink in.

Then Gazzy hollered, "Iggy! Dylan! Fang's room! *Now!*"

"*Oh, my God!*" Nudge yelled, bouncing on her heels in excitement. "Oh, my God, *Angel!*"

"Did I hear 'Angel'?" Dylan asked, poking his head around the door.

"What?" Iggy demanded, coming on Dylan's heels and skidding to a stop in the hallway.

Gazzy read the blog comment aloud. As before, we were all quiet for a bit as Iggy and Dylan processed the information.

And then—without any warning—we all leaped up, screaming and yelling and hugging until our voices and arms gave out. Nudge was sobbing; Gazzy kept chanting "My sister's alive! My sister's alive!" over and over; Iggy was laughing maniacally; Dylan stayed next to me, grinning, while I acted like my usual stoic, leaderly self (read: sobbing just as hard as Nudge). And in the middle of all of us, Fang was smiling with an abandon that I'd never seen him show before.

For the first time in my life, I saw tears in Fang's eyes.

He squeezed my hand, and I knew right then that regardless of traps, regardless of risks, everything was going to be all right. The flock was about to be complete again.

Our baby was coming home.

50

THE VERY NEXT morning, all six of us—Gazzy, Nudge, Iggy, Fang, Dylan, and I—got up bright and early to leave on the first rescue mission in . . . how many months? Three? Four? Man, that might have been the longest period of time without a rescue since Jeb had whisked us away from the School. Impressive.

We didn't bother telling the principal or teachers at Newton the small, insignificant fact that their precious bird kids were leaving on an impromptu trip to California, possibly never to return. After all, I've said it before and I'll say it again: We've spent our entire, unglamorous lives not being controlled by grown-ups. Why start now?

"Okeydokey," I said to myself, stuffing another bag of beef jerky into a backpack. "Provisions, check. Clothes, check. Enough explosives to pose a legitimate threat to multiple small countries"—I eyed the duffel bags that Gazzy and Iggy had packed—"check. Destination"—I glanced at the printed-out sheet with a marked map, courtesy of Mazin Nourahmed the Helpful (and Possibly Evil?) Blog Commenter—"check."

Six backpacks were laid out before me, for six bird kids. Usually I'd have to pack one for Total, too, but following my recommendation, he'd agreed to stay behind for this one. I'd arranged for him to stay with Akila. If this mission didn't go well, I didn't want his canine ladyfriend to end up a widow.

"Ready?" Fang asked, sliding his arms through the straps of his backpack and giving me a warm, excited, anxious look—a look that betrayed way more emotion than I was used to seeing Fang display.

"Yup. Let's bust this joint," I said. Nudge and Gazzy exchanged smiles—we all had the same feeling about this mission. *Just like old times.*

Except, of course, this wasn't old times, or just any mission. It was Angel. And it was probably a trap. And even if we did somehow manage to find her, she might not be as okay as we were all desperately hoping she was. A lot can happen to a seven-year-old girl all alone at a School.

I let out a long breath, my hands shaking as I fumbled with my bag's zipper. *Stay positive. She is alive.*

"It's okay," said a familiar voice beside me. Dylan. "We'll find her."

I turned to face him. He looked serious and sincere. A lump suddenly formed in my throat, and I wanted to hug him. But Fang was right behind me, so I just nodded, knowing that Dylan understood, and praying hard that he was right.

I hoisted my backpack into the proper position for flight, looking over my shoulder at Fang as I did so. We exchanged a brief look, I did a silent head count, and then he said, "Okay! Everybody ready?"

"*Ready!*" the flock shouted in unison. Then, with Fang leading the way, we all kicked off the ground and soared into the bright blue sky.

Please be okay, Angel. We're coming.

51

IT WAS THE beginning of the end, but not the end that Angel expected.

When she awoke, her lungs were screaming. She thought she saw a blurry flash, and then the image of a giant, belching fireball exploding behind her damaged eyes, and she cried out in terror.

Another vision of the apocalypse. It had to be. There was nothing else that sent hot panic surging through her like that. The very essence of chaos, fire and brimstone. The violent sound of the earth being savagely reclaimed for nature.

It wasn't supposed to be like this, Angel thought. *When the end comes, I'm supposed to be with Max. With my flock. When we die, we will be together.*

She had just sucked in a ragged, hot breath of stinking smoke when she realized she was still in the lab, clamped to the table, her limbs splayed out as if she were a butterfly on display. For a fleeting second the surrounding madness was drowned out by the deafeningly quiet memory of the whisper-sound of her feathers drifting to the lab floor, the endless flow of tears running down her face. After that, she'd passed out.

Now she coughed weakly into her shoulder, but she couldn't seem to take in enough oxygen as she choked on the smoke that was forcing itself under the door and into the room where she lay, alone.

Outside the door she heard muffled shouts and frantic footsteps.

"It's time!" Angel was able to make out a woman's voice yelling. "It's really happening!"

Somewhere an alarm was triggered, and the high, plaintive cry drowned out much of the chaos. The door of the lab burst open then, and someone was banging through cupboards while someone else rifled through papers and clanged metal objects around.

They were ignoring Angel completely.

"Help," she croaked. "Dr. Martinez?"

"Take everything!" a voice Angel didn't recognize commanded to someone else. "The 99% Plan is in effect!"

For the first time since the operation, Angel became dimly aware of being able to see movement, but she didn't have time to wonder about what was happening to her eyesight. She was wired to survive, and focused on trying to decipher who was in the room with her, and what they were doing. She fumbled wildly, trying to figure out how she might unlock her clamps, anything to free herself. But Angel could only make out blurred fractions of light, movements masked in smoke.

"Help," she said again, coughing.

But no one answered, and the footsteps were already fading away. And then, over the wail of the alarm, she couldn't hear any more voices. Beyond the wall of smoke, she couldn't breathe.

No! her brain shouted, rebelling against the inevitable. *No, I will not die like this, alone in smoky darkness. Not after the hell I have been through.*

She began to fight then, really fight, even though every single muscle and bone in her body ached.

"You can't leave me here!" Angel screeched with fury and despair to the empty walls around her. "I'm human, do you hear me? It *hurts*!"

She sobbed as she thrashed against the clamps and felt the cords digging into her flesh. But no matter how hard she struggled, she was trapped.

Smoke filled Angel's lungs and she hacked wildly, gasping. The sound of the alarm seemed to ricochet around her brain.

It's over, she thought with a sense of crushing defeat. Images of a giant, unstoppable wave gathering speed tormented her as she started to lose consciousness. *For once, the freaks were right: It's the end.*

Book Three
THE END

52

"HOW MUCH LONGER?" Gazzy asked breathlessly, catching a small updraft and banking left till he was flying next to me. He was grinning, but his face was lined with strain, and he looked more determined than I'd ever seen him.

"Just a little bit more," I said. Less than five hours after leaving Oregon, we had begun to near the facility, which, according to our source, was in Death Valley—so close to the School that Jeb had taken us from that I almost had a memory-induced panic attack.

"Days? Hours? Minutes?" Gazzy pressed.

"In fifteen minutes we should be within a mile radius. Then we find the place, touch down, do some recon."

"And then find Angel," he said fervently. "And spring

her out of there. And do serious damage to whoever's had her."

I winced. "Gaz..."

"I know, I know," the Gasman said. "Could be a trap, she might not be there, I get it. But still. She could be alive, Max!"

"Yeah, sweetie," I said, grinning. "She could be."

I happened to look over and meet Dylan's eyes, which were as blue as the sky we were flying in. He hadn't said much this morning. Actually, he hadn't been saying all that much since Fang had returned. Mr. Discuss Everything was suddenly how Fang used to be. Meanwhile, Fang was now talking and emoting and expressing more than ever before. It was like the two of them had switched personalities.

"Yo, up ahead!" Fang said suddenly. "I see something!"

Nudge nodded excitedly. "It looks like a cluster of buildings!"

We all—well, except Iggy—concentrated on the ground, letting our raptor vision focus in on what indeed appeared to be a cluster of buildings, some of which were made of boring gray and black stone, others of brick and gleaming one-way glass. The buildings were arranged in the shape of a *T*, and to be honest, they looked like they could hold pretty much *anything* institutional and uninteresting. A coat-hanger factory. Whatever.

Except for the fact that they were in the middle of nowhere, with no cities, towns, or even houses in sight.

And their location corresponded perfectly with the map we'd been given online.

"This is it," Fang muttered. "Circle down."

As we drifted back down to earth, Dylan moved closer to me. "Ready to beat up some whitecoats?" he said over the noise of the wind.

"Always," I said. And I was glad he was with me.

The six of us landed among a sea of small desert shrubs and immediately sank down to their height, keeping low. Then we got in a huddle to go over the plan for the umpteenth time.

"Okay, so first Max and I scout the place," said Fang. "Look for possible cracks in the armor, etc. If we don't come back within a half hour—"

"We fly to Badwater Basin," Iggy interrupted. "Then we wait for three days. Then, if you're still not back—"

"We absolutely *do not* barge in there and attempt to rescue you," Nudge deadpanned, repeating the words I'd drilled into all of them over and over again. "We act like sensible, self-preserving mutants and head back to Oregon."

"Good," I said. "Anybody have a problem with the plan?"

They all shook their heads no. Except Dylan. I knew he wanted to go with me, knew he was miffed, or peeved, or maybe even furious that I'd asked him to stay with the others. He'd bought my explanation—that they would need another good fighter with them, and that Dylan, out of all of us, was the least well known to the inner circle of crazed maniacs who seemed to chase us everywhere we went. He'd bought it. But he wasn't happy about it.

I looked at Fang. "You ready?"

He nodded, his eyes burning into mine, reading me, knowing my needs and my history and, it seemed, even my thoughts.

We'd just bent our knees and were about to take off together when Iggy yelled, "Wait!"

We all turned to him, instantly on the alert. "Fire," he warned. "I smell smoke."

"Smoke?" I glanced around, not seeing or smelling anything other than the undisturbed buildings and the clear, sunny day. "From where?"

Wordlessly, he pointed in the direction of the facility we were about to break into, and then the breeze changed and I smelled it, too: smoke. Lots of it.

Little did we know then that the 99% Plan was in effect . . . just a little bit ahead of schedule.

53

THE SMOKE LED us right to the burning building, which was eerily hushed, with only the crackling sound of dying flames, and no signs of life anywhere at first glance. No panicked refugees, no firefighters—just a red-hot shell.

When the fire had finally died down enough for us to safely explore the inside of the smoking facility, we stepped gingerly through the wreckage. Everything was horribly, deathly silent.

My intestines sank down to my shoes.

Marks from the fire had streaked the walls—or what remained of them—with gray and black. The stench of smoke permeated the dry air completely, scorched metal lay heaped where foundations used to be, and machinery that I recognized as mutant-testing equipment lay blackened and twisted in the rubble.

I swallowed. *Time to be a leader, Max.*

"Okay, everybody," I said, coughing against the thick air. "Search everything."

There was a huge crash then, as part of the floor above us gave way and a large piece of lab equipment fell through near to where we stood. Gazzy giggled nervously, at home in the destruction despite the underlying worry on his face.

"But *be careful*," I continued. "The roof could collapse at any second. Pay special attention to the part that wasn't destroyed—the eastern side. Angel could be in there."

Maybe. Hopefully. God, if she was in the section of buildings we were standing in . . . *Well, I would still want to find her,* I thought grimly. *Still want to take her body home.*

Carefully we picked our way toward the far side—the eastern side—through a doorway that had been stripped of its actual door.

I nearly threw up when I stepped over a partially melted plastic Kanine Kamper. Were we too late? Had we come this close only to miss saving Angel from a horrible death by—what, minutes?

My heart was shriveling, but I kept picking my way through the demolished building, opening every door, trudging down passages that led to the smell of fire and combustibles and sickening chemicals.

And fear. It hung in the air, thicker than smoke.

I don't want to describe the sick things we saw, experiments on...some kind of life-form...that had clearly failed. Everything that might have been alive was now dead from smoke inhalation, including a couple of whitecoats.

"How did the whole thing go up so quickly?" Dylan asked me. We were in the process of searching a lab that was filled with large machinery and operating tables. The sights made me physically ill. "I've been trying to work it out. It ate through the brick in, what? Ten minutes? And it was a scientific laboratory. Didn't they have some kind of fire-safety procedure?"

"Maybe they didn't *want* to stop it," Fang answered from across the room. He gestured at a utility closet, at a pile of overturned metal jugs inside. They reeked of gas fumes.

I heard Nudge gasp from another doorway and ran to her side, my adrenaline rushing.

"Max, why are they in a circle like that?" she whispered, her bottom lip quivering.

A strangled moan escaped my lips when I saw what she had found: the still smoking bodies in the lab, dozens of them, slumped against one another, arranged in a circle, just like Nudge had said. Like they'd been sitting down to tea, or a game of telephone. Like they'd died en masse.

My throat was dry and my mind was whirring.

We'd tried to get inside when we'd first seen the smoke, but the doors had all been bolted.

What had seemed like an abandoned building had been packed with people.

What had seemed like an accident reeked of purposeful destruction.

We'd been there for the fire. We'd watched the whole thing happen. No one had run outside.

I shivered, understanding the horrific implications. They'd *wanted* to die like this. This place was making my soul hurt.

"Max."

It was Dylan who'd spoken. He was down the hall.

"Yeah?" I forced the word out of my mouth, peeled my gaze away from the awful sight of the bodies before me. "Did you find something?"

"I . . . I think so." His tone was hollow.

I swallowed. I couldn't bear to find definitive evidence that we'd lost Angel. Not again. Not after we'd had so much hope.

Reluctantly, I came up beside Dylan. My eyes followed his gaze to the slick metal operating table in front of him. There were four clamps on it, in the corners, for restraining limbs.

Caught in one of the clamps were two soft, downy, white feathers.

"No," I choked out, my knees buckling.

Faintly, I heard the flock gathering behind me: Nudge's intake of breath, Gazzy's moan of pain, Iggy's hiss, and Fang's teeth gnashing together. But I couldn't stop staring, horrified, at the feathers in the clamp.

You'd think it couldn't get any worse, after that.

But it did, of course. Because right then, we heard the sweet, sociopathic voice that would give us all nightmares for the rest of our lives.

"May I help you?"

54

IT TOOK ME about zero point three seconds to recognize the man standing before us: Mark. The once manic leader of the Doomsday Group. Someone I hadn't seen since Paris, since Angel disappeared. I was pretty sure he was responsible for that whole bloody nightmare.

"Hello, children," Mark said languidly. His entire body was covered with horrible burns, and his clothes were scorched and torn to the point of falling apart.

"*You*," Gazzy spat. His voice was shaking. "You're the one from the tunnels! *You hurt me and my sister!*"

We were all glaring daggers at Mark, but despite his burns and the excruciating pain he must've been in, his expression was one of dreamy bliss, and that was what truly scared me, what made the hair on my arms stand up and my blood run cold. Angry people I can deal with; I can handle rage with a quick fight. Insane people are much more terrifying. They're totally unpredictable.

"Just say the word," Fang said to me under his breath. My hands clenched into fists as I prepared to kill the man who had taken Angel from us, to tear him limb from limb. Dylan readied himself beside me.

"I'm not a threat, children," Mark said, still wearing that crazed, happy expression of his. He took a step forward and the six of us stepped back instinctively. "This was all for you. At last, it's begun." Mark paused, looking bemusedly around at the destruction, at the burned wreckage, as if not really understanding what had happened. "It's begun," he repeated. Another beatific smile. "My work here is done. I've saved the planet. Saved it, protected it for the select few. And you, my friends, will benefit."

"What are you *talking* about?" I demanded. If there's anything worse than a psychopath, it's one who thinks he's doing his evil deeds for a good reason. "How has all this"—I waved my arm to encompass our surroundings—"saved the planet? How was what you did in Paris *protecting the planet*?" I was shrieking in his face, rage dripping from my every word.

His eyes were peaceful. "You'll see," he assured me. He glanced down at his burned arms, the flesh flayed open and raw. He didn't seem to be feeling anything. He looked up, his eyes coming to rest on one shattered window. Its wire-embedded glass had been twisted outward by some explosive force. Mark examined it: a novelty. Then he turned back to us. "You'll see," he repeated. "The contagion has been unleashed. Now all will come to pass. And you'll thank me for it."

"Not likely," I said, advancing toward him. "The only contagion I'm aware of is you and your insane cult. Now, if you don't tell us where you took—"

"Take care of the earth, my children," Mark interrupted, still smiling.

And then he threw himself out the window.

We have lightning-fast reflexes, but none of us got to him in time—it had happened so fast, with no warning. Horrified, we ran to the window and looked out. We weren't up very high, but he'd landed on a pile of broken concrete. Shafts of rusty rebar stuck up at different angles, one of them directly through Mark's throat.

He still had that pleasant smile on his face, but his eyes stared blankly into nothing.

"Unhhh," Nudge groaned, and then vomited on the floor at my feet.

As I rubbed her back, I felt warm hands on my shoulders, and for a second I couldn't tell if it was Dylan or Fang. Then Fang moved into my line of sight, scowling. It was Dylan who stood behind me.

I stared down at Mark's body and felt bile rising in my

own throat. "Well, that's…that," I said shakily, moving away from the window.

"So, we continue searching for Angel?" Dylan asked quietly.

I nodded. "We *always* continue searching for Angel."

55

WE SEARCHED THE whole place, and my heart sank lower with every empty room. Not that the rooms were actually empty. They were full of the stuff of nightmares: blood-stained operating tables, cabinets full of horrifying tools, jars of specimens that made my stomach turn. Only Iggy would avoid having these appalling images seared into his brain. The rest of us would carry them forever, like scars.

Nudge reached out and took my hand, held it tightly as we looked at another huge jar holding a preserved experiment. *Oh, God.*

"Evil. So evil," I muttered, feeling heartsick.

This had to be where Angel had been kept captive, ever since Paris. I didn't say anything to the others, but a black fog was starting to shroud my aching heart. How could she have survived this? And if she had survived it, how would she ever recover? Not just physically, but emotionally. We'd already been through more than anyone should have to go through. What if she'd finally been pushed over the edge? What if she could never come back?

After yet another horrifying sight made me gag, I leaned against the wall and rubbed my eyes, which stung from the lingering smoke and chemical fumes. My throat was scratchy and dry, and it ached from the effort of suppressing my cries of shock and horror.

"She's not here," Gazzy said tonelessly, sitting down on a broken beam. "Or if she's here, she's part of the ashes." His voice broke.

"Let's start over again, from the first building," Dylan said, squeezing Gazzy's shoulder. He sounded tired but determined.

"No," said Fang. "We should take to the sky, do recon, and see if they left tracks—whoever escaped, I mean. She could be with them."

"You think some people escaped?" Nudge's face was drawn.

Fang nodded. "Someone always escapes."

This had all been for nothing. My baby was still gone.

Don't give up, Max.

My Voice was very, very faint. It had never before sounded like it was talking to me from as far away as the moon; I almost thought I'd imagined it.

Then I saw something through the dust on the floor. I

pushed aside some charred beams and uncovered a metal trapdoor, maybe two feet by two feet and padlocked from the outside.

"Nudge?" I whispered.

Closing her eyes, she swept her sensitive fingers over the lock several times. I didn't know how or why she could affect metal with her touch, but I was glad she could. Her fingers trembled with both effort and emotion, and we all clung to the hope that there might be one more place we hadn't looked.

The lock sprang open in her hand, and we yanked the doors open.

A narrow metal staircase led down into darkness.

I went down first, my senses screaming with alertness. It took my eyes a couple of seconds to adjust to the lack of light, but at my first quick scan, we seemed to be in a small room.

An *empty* room.

I felt a terrible pain in my chest as my heart constricted with grief. There was nowhere else to look. Angel was either dead or being rushed to another secret facility, and I knew she wouldn't be able to withstand this torture until we could find her again.

The tears I had been holding back during our search suddenly started streaming down my face. I couldn't breathe. I wanted to fly out of there and never come back. Let the world take care of itself from now on. I was done.

As I turned to rush out, my eyes fell on a small back

room, behind the stairs we had just come down. I reached the doorway in two strides.

A feathery, dirty heap was strapped to a table in one cold corner.

"Angel?" I whispered, not letting myself believe it could be her. We knew there were other winged kids out there. It would be too good to be true. . . .

I took a few more steps toward the figure, and then collapsed to the floor beside it. I knew that face, that hair, no matter how wrecked they had become.

Trust me, it's impossible to describe the rush that happens when your whole soul shifts, in an instant, from despair and loss to realizing that maybe it was all just a horrible lie, a nightmare—that hope is truly *alive.*

"Angel!" I cried, sobbing and stroking matted curls away from her grimy face, while Fang immediately started dismantling the clamps. *"Angel!* We're right here. We came to get you. Angel—wake up!"

I gently cradled her head, which lolled back. Was it really her? Or just . . . her body?

I got no response. As soon as Fang was finished with the clamps I gathered her up, and it felt like I was holding Styrofoam. There was hardly anything there, as if she hadn't eaten since Paris. Numerous puncture wounds dotted both arms. How many times could my baby be torn from me and survive it?

The massive tsunami wave of joy I'd felt moments earlier was already rushing back out to sea.

"Angel, please," I begged, cuddling her close. "Please be okay. We're all here now. Max, Fang, Iggy, Nudge, Gazzy, Dylan... we're all right here. You're safe. We're all together. Please, sweetie, please wake up." My words were coming in gasps.

Then—had I imagined it? Had her too-thin, too-light body shifted?

She made a tiny sound. Her eyelids fluttered.

"She's alive!" Gazzy's voice was hushed but thrilled.

A fierce joy swelled inside me. She was *alive*! She really was!

And she was going to stay that way, at least while I was on this planet. No matter what, I would never, ever let her out of my sight. We would never be separated again.

56

MY BRAIN WAS on a drunken loop of joy, disbelief, shock, ecstasy.

This is really my Angel, my own Angel....

The others crowded around and tried to touch and embrace her, so they, too, could truly believe what I was still trying to absorb. But I wouldn't let go of her.

"We need to get her out of here," Dylan instructed, gently pushing his way in close to help me lift her body. I hardly registered Fang's irritated look. Nothing in the world mattered to me at that moment except keeping my little girl safe with me.

I stood up and carried Angel upstairs, into the light. Someone had padlocked her in that underground room—there would have been no way for her to get out. Someone had left her there to die.

"Max?" Her voice was barely a breath.

"Yes, sweetie," I said, trying not to leak tears on her. "I'm here. We're going to get you somewhere safe, get you all patched up, good as new."

Her small head shook. "I'll never be as good as new," she whispered weakly. "They messed up my eyes. They clipped my wings."

"*What?*"

"I'll never fly again," she whimpered sadly. Tears slowly streaked the dirt on her face.

Quickly I traced down her primary feathers to her flight feathers, fanning them gently in my hand. They looked fine.

"No, your feathers are okay," I reassured her, understanding the kind of crazy confusion the whitecoats' drugs could cause. "You'll be fine—I promise. You'll be flying in no time. We'll take care of you."

Her eyes opened slightly and she looked into the sky, past my head. "They experimented on my eyes, Max."

A cold fist grabbed my heart and yanked. "What?"

"Like Iggy," she confirmed, and I was seized with fresh horror. "Jeb was here—he said it was for my own good." Her voice was weak—it was hard to make out what she was saying.

"Tell me, Angel," I said urgently, pulling Gazzy to my side. "Who is standing right next to me? *Tell me.* Don't tell me you're blind."

"I—I—" She blinked. And blinked again. We were all holding our breath. "My brother...Gazzy..." She breathed. "Is that you?"

Gazzy threw his arms around her and sobbed.

"Everything is kind of a blur," Angel whispered as Gazzy pulled away.

"Shh, sweetie," I said. "Don't try to talk. You're waking up from a drug-induced nightmare. We'll make sure you're okay. We're going to take you home now."

Again she shook her head, opened her eyes. She peered up at me anxiously, her eyes not quite focusing. "Max, your mom was there. I saw her. Dr. Martinez. She's...she's one of them."

I looked up to see the flock recoiling in shock.

"No, sweetie," I said, my mind reeling. "You've been hallucinating. Your feathers are fine, and my mom isn't one of the baddies. It was all just weird hallucinations."

Angel shook her head. "No. Your mom was there. She helped them. Dr. Martinez is on their side."

57

I TRIED TO keep my emotions under control as we flew home, but sometimes I could barely see through the tears.

Angel weighed so little that it was no problem for Dylan, Iggy, Fang, and me to take turns carrying her on the flight. We also picked up Total on the return trip. I knew he'd want to see Angel right away, and I was right—I'd never heard him bark so wildly with joy.

As soon as Angel was settled—cleaned up and in fresh clothes, but still pale and worn out—I left her sleeping peacefully, with Nudge and Gazzy in charge and Total curled up at her side. I needed to be alone in the woods for a minute to get my emotions under control—otherwise I'd be a crying mess when Angel was finally ready to talk about what had happened.

So it wasn't necessarily the best timing when Fang crept up quietly behind me, just like he always used to, and scared the stuffing out of me.

"We need to talk. About you. And me."

I could feel the heat rising to my cheeks. "There *is* no you and me, per your instructions," I said, my jaw clenching.

"I don't know about that," he said.

"Oh, please. You *left*," I said accusingly. "*Twice*, actually. You threw any *us* we had in my face! Then you decided to get all hot and heavy with Maya." That last part came out before I could stop it, and I cringed, remembering what Ari had said.

"Maya's dead," Fang said tensely, confirming what I already knew. I winced at the grief in his voice. "And this isn't about her. It's about the connection you and I have— will *always* have, no matter what." I opened my mouth to retort, but nothing came out, so Fang forged right on, breaking my heart with his honesty.

"I heard a Voice, Max," he said, gripping my arm, pulling me closer, "and it told me I needed to come home to you. Even though I had to practically *walk* the whole way. Even though I was close to dying. I came back. To you. And I wanted to tell you—maybe I never told you very clearly before…"

My heart was racing so fast I thought I was having a heart attack.

"I wanted to tell you that I—"

"Stop!" I cried, putting my hands over my ears. "Just *don't*, okay?"

But Fang looked determined, and there was only one thing to do when he looked like that. I took off.

If I pour on the speed, I can hit almost three hundred miles per hour while flying—faster than any recombinant life-form I've ever heard about. Faster than anyone. Except Fang.

I was probably already a couple of miles away, still sniveling and cursing, when I felt a hand grab my sneaker. He stayed with me, matching me stroke for stroke without releasing his death grip on my ankle.

Finally it was too hard to stay balanced, so I put on the brakes. I banked steeply and whirled around to face him.

"Fang, I can't hear this right now!" I shouted, tears streaming down my face. "My life is hard and confusing enough without you making it harder! Everything's just really, you know, *complicated*, and..." I trailed off, thinking of the complicated things in my life. The other complicated *someone*.

"I'm not trying to make it harder or more confusing," Fang said quietly, smiling that lopsided smile of his. Warm emotion showed in his black eyes, and for a minute I actually had to concentrate on staying airborne. "I'm trying to tell you what you already know. I just...*need* you. We need each other."

"But *I* just can't do *this*." I flailed my arms around, indicating whatever *this* was—encompassing everything. "With you. Not now, not *today*, not after everything we've been through with Angel, so..." I swallowed, trying to ignore my stupid heart. "Just don't say any more," I whispered. "Please."

But if I could hear the catch in my voice, I knew Fang had picked up on it, too.

He had moved closer. We were nose to nose now, our wings almost overlapping as each stroke took us up ten feet, then down again. We'd been flying together our whole lives, and keeping in perfect rhythm was second nature to us. My arms were crossed over my chest, my elbows almost brushing against him, and Fang reached out and held my arms, below my shoulders. He let his thumbs brush against my skin, slowly.

I shivered. Fang's touch was so familiar. How many times had he done this? Old times and new all jumbled together. Emotions and memories became indecipherable. The only thing I knew was that we'd grown and changed. It was almost like he was a new Fang. I felt almost like a new Max. Could we still...fit together?

"Max." He said my name like it was a life raft. Like it was a religion. His warm fingers stroked up and down my arms.

"What?" I whispered. Or had I even said it aloud? I didn't know what to do, so I stared into his eyes for the answer. And I let them rest there. I didn't want to be the first to look away.

I reached out and put my hands on his shoulders, felt his strong, light bones under his skin. I remembered what he had carved into a cactus once.

MAX + FANG — 4EVER.

58

TEARS POURED DOWN Dylan's face. He dashed them away angrily with the back of his hand, flapping his wings powerfully and putting as much distance between himself and *them* as he could.

He'd been in a tree a good half mile away from them—not *spying*, just...*seeing*. Seeing his past going up in flames, his future crumbling into dust. He wasn't about to stick around to watch Max and Fang finally have their little private reunion party.

He'd thought what he and Max had was starting to grow into something...real. She'd let him sleep in her room. And that night in the tree house...He remembered the feel of Max's skin under his fingertips, her wildly tangled hair brushing against his cheek, the look she gave him just before their lips met....

He could live and die inside that single look.

Dylan shook his head, flapped his wings harder. Faster. He took the next turn too tightly and lost control, dropping hundreds of feet before he could level himself. He saw the forest ahead. Tall trees, growing thickly together. He narrowed his eyes and dove down.

He wove crazily in and out of the trees, at top speed. He scared birds, startled a group of deer, and still he went as fast as possible, so fast that the wind would dry his tears.

Again and again he flipped sideways to fit through narrow openings. His sneakers smacked against tree trunks. Bark raked the skin on his hands and face raw. Branches caught at his feathers, and he felt some get yanked out, but he didn't even wince.

It felt good, the pain. He wanted more.

All this time he'd tried to be good. He'd followed the rules—or at least the rules *Max* had set. He had learned to fly and to fight, had followed her lead. He had given her space, and then pressed a little closer when she seemed to want it. He'd done everything he was supposed to, *when* he was supposed to. He had thought if he could just be *perfect*, Max would love him.

But she loved Fang instead. *Fang*, who seemed to break every rule in the book. Dylan set his jaw. *Fine*, he thought. *She wants a bad boy like Fang, I can do that.*

Bam!

He brought his feet down, hard, on the roof of a car that was driving toward town, making a huge dent.

Bam! Bam! Bam! Three more cars suffered the same fate. Dylan felt a rush of thrill and fear: This was the best he'd felt since Fang had come back.

On the next car, Dylan dropped down even lower. *Snap!* One quick kick took the side mirror right off. *Crash!* A rear windshield was smashed to smithereens.

It was an incredible feeling of power, a power he'd never felt before.

He rose a bit and banked sideways dramatically, hearing car horns honking, people shouting. He wheeled around the store on the corner, then swooped down and grabbed the store's banner with one hand, ripping it from where it had hung across the sidewalk. It landed on a car driving underneath it, causing the driver to lose control and crash into a telephone pole.

But Dylan was already halfway down the street, ripping street signs from their posts and hurling them like Frisbees. People were yelling at him now. A baseball whistled past his head. He could hear sirens behind him.

Over and over, he dropped down suddenly, kicked over a mailbox, a trash can, a trellis. But the pain in his chest was returning. He reached up and ripped the electrical wires strung along the street from their poles. Sparks shot everywhere as the live wires fell to the ground, igniting the bulging trash bags that lined the curb.

At last Dylan realized he was weeping again. He could hardly see. What was happening to him? Nothing was making sense—least of all his behavior.

He rose gracefully, powerfully into the air, leaving behind a roiling fire that was beginning to streak through a destroyed neighborhood.

This isn't the answer, Dylan, said his Voice. *You know what your job is. You know what you have to do.* Dylan shook his head, as if he could shake the Voice loose, make it go away forever.

A thought flitted through his brain like the light fingers of a practiced thief. He turned around slowly and tasted bile in his throat.

No. He *couldn't*. Could he?

It was the answer to so many of his problems. What he *couldn't* do was what the science teacher had demanded on that awful day in the lab at school—he couldn't turn Fang over for the whitecoats to experiment on, no matter how much he hated him at that moment. He would never condemn anyone to such a fate.

But if he didn't turn Fang in, someone else would. And if what Dr. Williams had said was true, they would hurt—possibly kill—Max as a result.

He couldn't let that happen.

Dylan's mind spun. Maybe this awful thought . . . maybe this was the *right* thing to do in the end. It would spare Fang from a horrible life of tests and scalpels and torture.

It would save Max's life. She would be grateful; maybe she'd even come to love him for it...someday.

Dylan swallowed. The Voice was right. He *did* know what he had to do. He had known all along.

He had to kill Fang.

59

"OH, MY GOD, it's Dylan."

My head swiveled sharply at Gazzy's words and I practically ran to where he sat on the couch. He was pointing at the TV screen.

"What 'oh, my God'?" I demanded. "What 'Dylan'?"

"He's...he's...gone wacko," said Gazzy.

I turned my attention to the news broadcast, which was showing a grainy, shaky cell phone video...of a bird kid rampaging through town. My mouth dropped open as I saw *Dylan*—and he was totally, prosecutably recognizable as Dylan—smashing windows, ripping down signs, kicking cars, knocking over mailboxes.

"It doesn't seem like him at all," said Gazzy. "He's

always so laid back. Maybe it's, like, a clone or something?" he offered.

"No," I murmured, anxiously watching the screen. "No, I think it's really him." But why was he on this insane destructive streak? What had happened since I last saw him? I tried to think when that was....

He'd been with me all day, right up until—*oh*. Suddenly it all became horribly clear, and my stomach clenched. Dylan had been near the door when I'd gone outside to be alone. He must have seen Fang follow me, which meant he'd seen Fang and me fly off, out of earshot of the house.

What else had he seen?

"This is all my fault," I muttered, grabbing my jacket. "I'm going to find him."

Before Gazzy could say anything, I'd leaped off our balcony and was streaking toward town.

60

I WAS AT the edge of town before I realized that I had no idea what I was going to say to Dylan when I found him.

Dylan had had my back when I didn't really have anyone else, and he was the last person in the world I wanted to hurt. He was...Well, he was a great guy, and I knew exactly how much he cared about me. He'd worn his heart on his wing, and he deserved honesty from me in return.

But what could I say to him? What could I offer him? What could I promise? How could I know what to say when I hardly even knew what to *feel* these days?

God help me.

I kept myself high enough in the sky so that people wouldn't necessarily spot me right away. But I could still see everything, and I almost skidded to a halt when I saw firsthand the damage Dylan had done.

The town was in chaos. It looked like a tornado had streaked through, wrecking everything in its path. There were dented cars stopped on Main Street, store owners talking angrily to police, people sweeping up glass and reattaching signs. It was like Dylan had woken up today and decided to play Godzilla.

I let out a slow breath, understanding the implication: The measure of damage that Dylan had caused was probably about equal to the amount of pain he might be in right now.

Because of me.

My heart in my throat, I kept scanning the streets, but what I didn't see was Dylan. I went high, way high, to give myself a broader view, but saw not a feather. I scanned treetops, the roofs of buildings, other places suitable for hiding out and seething, but he had disappeared.

And when he came back—*if* he came back—how would things be then? Would he still be the sweet, vulnerable Dylan I had begrudgingly come to rely on, to even *like*?

To *more than* like. I couldn't admit to myself just what that feeling was, but it was something that had started to work its way deep inside me.

I'd been trying for so long to ignore his adoring looks, to distance myself and push him away.

So if I'd finally succeeded, why did it hurt so much?

61

HE'S HOME.

That was my first thought when I was rudely jolted out of a restless sleep that night. For the second time in just a couple of weeks, Iggy's alarm system was sending wails and automated warning messages through the house in the middle of the night.

Be angry, I told myself as I bolted from my bed. *He shouldn't have taken off like that, shouldn't have caused all that damage. You're furious.* But I couldn't stop the feelings of relief and elation that swept through me as I headed for the door.

"What is it? Who's attacking us?" Gazzy yelled from his room. "Should I bring the bombs?"

"Max?" Angel whimpered, stumbling out of my way sleepily as I rounded the corner and ran down the hall.

"It's okay, Angel. Everything's fine. Don't worry, guys," I yelled over my shoulder as I started to unbolt the locks. "Iggy! Cut the alarm! It's just Dyl—"

I breathlessly threw open the door, and a sea of glowing red eyes peered at me out of the frigid darkness.

Behind me, Nudge sucked in a breath—there were *a lot* of eyes, and they were feral, bloodthirsty: Erasers.

I swallowed, my words dying on my lips. *"Of course,"* I muttered, trying not to show how overwhelmed I was by the sheer numbers, how unprepared I'd just been caught. I had *opened the door* to these mongrels, without any weapon or plan. I had practically invited them in.

I cleared my throat and stepped right out onto the porch. I could hear breathing and shuffling in the darkness, animal sounds that sent chills down my spine. You'd think I would be used to it by now. "So," I said loudly, "is there a specific reason you flea-bitten wolves are attacking? Or is it just my lucky day?"

"Just your lucky day, sis."

I knew that voice: bitter, deep, like a bunch of rocks being rattled in a can. *Ari.*

The crowd of Erasers parted so he could walk through, and he stopped just ten feet from the bottom of the stairs. My stomach turned somersaults—somehow he looked even bigger and wolfier. Maybe he had been "enhanced" some more.

"This is the end, Max," Ari said, stepping into the beam of the porch light and showing his yellow fangs. "I promise."

"I stopped believing your promises a long time ago," I said. I felt just a tiny bit sad, remembering the cute kid he had once been. My half brother.

The other Erasers were moving forward now, ever so slowly. Every single one of them was staring fixedly in the same direction. At the same person.

And it wasn't me.

"We're here for *you*, Fang," Ari said, looking into the hallway behind me and grinning toothily as he cracked his meaty, hairy knuckles. "We're here to kill you, and trust me—this is one fight you bird kids can't win."

Fang came out to stand beside me, his fists clenched, his face tight with anger. "I wouldn't bet on that."

"Your funeral," Ari said, shrugging. He held up one hairy fist, ready to give the signal to his army.

I tensed, settling my weight as I prepared to leap off the porch. I didn't know if these Erasers could fly, but regardless, I was not going to start this fight on my feet. I was ready. I'd been ready for this for a long time. And my plan was to ignore any and all pain until every Eraser was gone.

But you know, things can always, always, take a turn for the worse.

"Just say the word, *Dad*," Ari called out.

So there you go.

62

OUT OF THE shadows stepped the one, the only, the despicable Jeb. And get this—he was actually wearing a white lab coat. And a small frown.

"Wait, Ari," Jeb said firmly. "I need to explain things first."

For a moment, I thought Ari was going to ignore the command and just attack us anyway—that was what he would have done just a few months earlier. He hated and resented Jeb as much as he did us.

But after a moment's hesitation, he nodded and slowly lowered his fist, though he never took his rabid eyes from Fang's face.

Jeb moved closer to the porch. I kept my face expressionless, staying in battle mode. My muscles were coiled, my heart was pumping, and every sense was hyperalert. I knew that my flock—even Angel, who was still so fragile—was ready, just like I'd trained 'em to be. Just like Jeb had trained me.

"Max, Fang," Jeb said, sounding urgent, "I need you to understand."

Behind him, Ari shifted, and all of the red Eraser eyes in the darkness shifted along with him. They were muttering now, and I heard twigs snapping as they moved around impatiently. I had no idea how long Ari or Jeb could keep them in check.

"Save it," I said, crossing my arms over my chest. "We don't need to listen to any more of your lies."

"No, but you *do* need to know the truth, Max. The truth about why Fang must die."

I laughed coldly. "That actually sounds like something we absolutely don't need to hear," I replied. "It sounds totally irrelevant, actually. Because Fang isn't going to die. You may have created us, Jeb, but you do *not* get to decide when we die. The only expiration date that's approaching is yours, the second you try to get any closer to him."

I saw the rest of the flock out of the corner of my eye, moving to stand next to me on the porch in support. Iggy stepped protectively in front of Fang and crossed his arms.

"Max, you don't understand." Jeb looked up at me. "I don't *want* Fang to die, any more than you do. But he *needs* to. If the earth is going to survive, *Fang must die.*"

Fang stepped forward from the shadows and let out a long breath. "Go on," he said, watching Jeb steadily.

I reached out and took his hand, holding it tight.

"When you were in Dr. Gunther-Hagen's lab," began Jeb, "he took samples of your tissue, did all sorts of tests on you, on your skin and muscles and organs. And eventually he made an amazing discovery. Fang, your DNA is *indestructible*. Infinitely regenerative."

"We all heal quickly," I ground out.

"No, Max, sweetie." Jeb shook his head slowly, ignoring the look on my face at the word "sweetie." "Fang is different. *His* DNA holds science's key to *immortality*."

Okay, I did not see *that* coming.

63

"I'M SO SORRY," Jeb said sincerely. "But now you understand why Fang must be eliminated."

I scowled at him. "No, actually, I can't say I do."

"If my DNA is so special, wouldn't that make me useful to keep alive?" asked Fang dryly. "For *science*?"

"Yes," Jeb agreed. "And that's exactly why Hans wants you alive—for that very reason. He intends to lock you up in his lab and put you into a permanent vegetative state. You understand what that means, don't you? You would be just a body, unable to move, think, eat, talk. A body that Hans intends to perform live experiments on *forever*."

I stared at Jeb in shock. Imagining Fang like that made me want to throw up.

Jeb paused, looking positively misty-eyed. "I myself would end your life right now, to save you from that endless nightmare. I created you, Fang. I could never let you endure that."

"He wouldn't have to endure anything," I said briskly, my mind racing. "We'd protect him. And if you loved us, you would, too. Take him somewhere safe. Somewhere Dr. Hans would never find him. We're good at running from idiots—as you well know, Jeb."

Jeb coughed and looked at the ground. When he looked back at me, his eyes were pleading, but apologetic. "It's not just Dr. Hans, Max. News travels fast in the world of science. Believe me, if I know of the discovery, many others do as well. And for something of this magnitude...They would come looking, more and more. You couldn't protect Fang forever"—his lips curled into a sad smile—"and I'm afraid that's how long you'd need to. What happens when you die, Maximum? Have you considered that? Who will protect Fang then?"

I clenched my fists but didn't answer. My mouth was dry, and I felt empty and hollow.

"I can take care of myself," Fang muttered. "Especially if I'm immortal."

Jeb shook his head sadly. "I'm afraid you're not immortal, Fang. We've determined that your DNA holds the secret to the pursuit of immortality. There's a difference. You're a critical link in the next great step in human evolution." He cleared his throat. "But this is not just about you, kiddo. This is bigger. It's about saving the whole world." Jeb looked at me. "It's what you've been preparing for all this time, Max."

"Wait—*what?*" Fang and I said at the same time.

My mind reeled as I tried to get a handle on this scenario. And Ari and the Erasers were having a harder time than I was—they were clearly bored out of their pea-sized minds and were visibly salivating, shivering with anticipation as they waited anxiously to tear into Fang.

Behind me, Nudge, Iggy, Gazzy, and Angel shifted their feet and unfurled their wings in case things got ugly in a hurry. It looked like they might.

Jeb went on, "Immortality might sound like a good thing, but as soon as it can be genetically engineered, we'll have a disaster on our hands. If people live forever, their numbers will increase exponentially—like a cancer metastasizing across the earth," Jeb said earnestly. "This is why I truly believe in the 99% Plan. The planet only has a chance if we take *people* out of the equation."

"Oh, come *on*," I scoffed, but Jeb was looking at Ari, who was moving toward his army of Erasers.

"It's okay," Fang said to me, trying to look reassuring. "They can't hurt me. I already cheated death once. I was pretty much resurrected after I was thrown from the cliff."

"Lose your God complex, my friend," Ari sneered. "When we get through with you, there won't be anything left to resurrect."

"I created you, Fang. I created a... well, a monster," Jeb said. "And now it's my duty to destroy you, before Dr. Hans and those like him can torture you forever. Before your DNA can destroy our planet. I'm so sorry, Fang!"

He nodded at Ari: *Take him out.*

64

BOOM!

I whipped around and saw that Gazzy had produced a bunch of homemade bombs—yes, from his *pajamas*—and started hurling them into the crowd. There were three fast explosions, and each one took out at least six Erasers. *That's my boy*, I thought proudly—

—and that thought cost me, because at that moment a huge, hard fist collided with my jawbone, rattling my brain and smashing my teeth together painfully. I rose into the air, fast, moving on instinct. As I took off I spit blood down on the crowd and moved my jaw to make sure it wasn't broken. I shook my head to clear it.

A hundred to six—by far the worst odds we'd ever faced. But I wasn't going down easily, and neither was

Fang—I'd make sure of that. I set my aching teeth and dive-bombed the mass of writhing, hairy bodies.

"Max, *duck*!"

I obeyed the order instantly. A bird kid streaked past me and rammed the Eraser I'd been aiming for. I had one startled second to glimpse sun-blond hair. Caribbean-blue eyes flashed at me and then turned their focus back to the battle.

"Dylan!" I half shrieked as I slammed my cupped hands over an Eraser's ears. His eardrums burst, and he howled in agony. "What the— Are you *insane*?"

"Later!" he yelled back. "I'm sorry!"

So am I, I thought, and then grabbed an Eraser's thick wrist and twisted, snapping it and stopping the Eraser before it got to Nudge. But three more were already after her. And three more were coming for *me*. I dodged them and did a quick spin to get my arm around one of their necks.

Suddenly I heard a loud roar: Ari had Fang in a choke hold. Fang's wings were pinned against his body, and Ari outweighed him by about a hundred pounds.

I headed toward them but as I did a claw raked my leg, making me gasp, and then several paws grabbed my ankle and pulled me downward. My sneakers hit dirt, and then I was whaling, punching, chopping, and kicking faster and harder than I ever had before. I had to: This fight mattered more than any other fight. Fang's life hung in the balance. It was do or die for real this time. Possibly both.

I dimly heard another battle cry and from the corner of my eye saw Dylan drop onto Ari, deflecting him away from Fang—a move that made my heart hurt.

Dylan soared upward, into the black sky, and Ari roared ferociously, following him with hatred in his eyes.

My breath caught in my throat: This would be a fight to the death. I knew it would.

65

MY IRRATIONAL DESIRE to join Dylan in combat with Ari was interrupted when a heavy hand on my shoulder made me spin, ready to attack.

Jeb quickly held up his hands.

"Don't *touch* me!" I spat.

His face fell, and in that moment, a thousand different memories flickered through my brain: Jeb taking care of us when we were little. Jeb leaving us. Jeb's face outlined by the fluorescent lights of the School. Jeb taking Angel, Jeb hurting us.

Jeb trying to kill Fang.

Harden your heart.

I put my fists up and narrowed my eyes.

"Max, please—just accept this." I still knew that voice

so well. "Fang has to die. One man sacrificed for the greater good—it's the right thing to do, sweetie."

Sweetie.

"Don't—you—ever—freaking—call—me—that!" I yelled, and then I kicked Jeb, the man who'd raised me, in the chest, hard enough that I heard multiple ribs cracking.

"Ohh," he moaned in surprise. He staggered backward, and then his face went white and he collapsed in a dead faint on the porch, his head hitting the ground with a thud.

I almost felt bad, almost moved to help him. Almost. Then I reminded myself that he wanted Fang dead.

I turned from Jeb's limp body and jumped right back into the fray without a second glance.

There were probably about forty Erasers left, plus Ari. We'd made huge progress, but the six of us were at our breaking point. All of us were bloodied, with black eyes, broken noses, split lips. My arms ached from punching and being punched, and the spot on my leg where the Eraser had clawed me was burning and hurting so badly that I couldn't put weight on it. There was no way we could last much longer.

Iggy was above me, with four Erasers circling him. It looked like he might have a broken ankle, which was preventing him from kicking out at them. All he could do was keep them away from the rest of us and hope to get in a lucky swing.

Gazzy was trying to keep the Erasers away from the house and distract the ones that were after Iggy, but one of his wings was slightly crumpled, and he couldn't get off the ground. Several Erasers had him pinned up against a tree at edge of the woods.

Nudge was screaming like a madwoman, pounding her sneaker into the face of an Eraser who held her by the ankle. But two more were coming up on her from behind.

I didn't know who to help first. And I had at least ten Erasers taking turns diving at me. As I smashed my fist into another one of their disgusting faces, I realized that I had just gotten Angel back...but I might be about to lose someone else.

Or everyone else.

66

CRIES AND GRUNTS overhead caught my attention. Dylan and Ari were both bloody and bruised, like the rest of us, and I couldn't even tell who was winning.

Dylan quickly landed five lightning-quick kicks to Ari's stomach, making him double over and wheeze. But Ari straightened almost immediately and swung a huge taloned paw through the air. I bit my lip as he sliced Dylan's side to ribbons, sending blood splashing thirty feet below to spatter the trampled, icy grass.

Ari had done that to Fang once. Fang had almost died.

I watched, holding my breath, as Dylan abruptly turned and hurtled toward a tree. He grabbed a strong branch, snapped it off as if it were a twig, and dove back toward Ari. Dylan swung the branch in a deadly arc...just as something collided with my head so hard that I gasped and stumbled. Immediately, I felt blood trickling down my cheek.

Watching the fight above had cost me.

I jumped to my feet and almost fell back down as a wave of dizziness hit me. Wiping blood out of my eyes, I made like a windmill, fists swinging in hard punches that jarred my shoulders, feet shooting out in kicks that were backed by every ounce of my weight. I could hardly tell which way was up or down, but I wouldn't give up. I could hear someone yelling in pain in the distance. My flock needed me.

"Don't give up, Nudge! Fang—help Gazzy and Iggy!"

I karate-chopped the throat of my umpteenth Eraser and screamed encouragement to my flock. *I won't let them die.* Whirling in a circle, I delivered a kick that snapped an Eraser's arm before shooting up onto the porch, where three more of them were trying to get into the house. There were Erasers *everywhere*.

I heard a bloodcurdling howl to my right. Dylan swung the tree branch again, and there was a sickening thud. Blood flew in all directions and Ari shrieked with murderous rage. He started to lunge toward Dylan but faltered suddenly, a fatal mistake.

My heart pounding, I watched Dylan swing the branch again, a cold, grim expression on his frighteningly beaten face. This time, the branch smashed into Ari's head. Ari's wings folded and he fell down, down, hitting the ground with bone-crunching force.

I stared at Ari's contorted, unnatural position—a position no living body could be in.

Dylan—alive and upright—floated slowly downward to land a couple of feet away from me on the porch. He looked dazed, and his shirt was shredded and so wet with blood that I couldn't tell what color it had been. His face was so beaten up that I mainly recognized him by his hair. He looked exhausted. Older.

"Max," he began, and gave a little cough. Then he collapsed at my feet.

"He's dead!" someone shouted. I didn't know who. I was too stunned by the horror of what I'd just witnessed.

But then, impossibly, miraculously, something else happened.

The Erasers suddenly went limp and crumpled lifelessly to the ground one by one.

67

DYLAN WATCHED WITH half-open eyes from the porch floor. *Out of batteries*, he thought. *Game over.* He was so dizzy, and not entirely sure he wasn't hallucinating. The fight with Ari had taken a lot out of him.

"What the—?" Iggy said mid-swing, as the fist he'd aimed at an Eraser's face connected with empty air.

"How come they're all down?" the Gasman asked exhaustedly. "Are they dead?"

"What happened?" Nudge asked, swaying slightly. All of the bird kids were more whipped, more damaged than Dylan had ever seen them.

"It's like...they were all linked," Fang said hoarsely. He wiped a hand under his nose, which was running with blood. Both of his eyes were swollen almost shut. "All connected, all 'wired' to their leader somehow. So if Ari died..."

"Then they would, too," finished Max. But her voice sounded funny, and she wasn't looking at the fallen Erasers, wasn't preoccupied with them the way everyone else was.

She was on her knees, looking at him, at *Dylan*, her expression afraid and grateful and so, so tender it made his heart thump wildly in his chest. She did care, then. She had to.

"Dylan, can you hear me?" she whispered urgently. Seeing his half-open eyes, she gave a sigh of relief. "I thought you were dead." She peeled his fingers away from his side.

He looked numbly down at the wound, where dark blood was still flowing freely from deep, agonizing slashes.

"Let's get you cleaned up." She tore one leg off her sweatpants and he watched her quick, capable fingers transform it into a bandage. He winced as she pressed it against him.

"At least it's over," Nudge said weakly. She smiled through a split and puffy lip, then sat down stiffly on a step. "Well, almost." She warily eyed Jeb's quietly groaning, semiconscious form, still lying awkwardly next to the porch where he'd passed out earlier, but no one said anything—they'd deal with him later.

"Cheers to that." The Gasman nodded and plopped down next to her with a sigh of relief, moving as if every muscle hurt.

And yet...for Dylan, it still wasn't over. Not even almost. Dylan, after all, still had a mission.

Though he and Ari had had the same goal, he hadn't trusted Jeb's motives, hadn't been sure that the rabid, enhanced wolves wouldn't go wild after Fang was dead and take out the entire flock. He'd needed to eliminate all threats to Max before he attempted his despicable mission. And he knew that once he had made up his mind, he had to be the one to do it.

Well, he thought, *now it's up to me alone.*

He had to be the one to kill Fang.

He struggled to his feet, conscious of Max's sweet, concerned eyes watching him carefully.

"I'm sorry, Max," he murmured, so softly that only she could hear.

And he whipped around, slamming his fist into Fang's already broken nose.

68

DYLAN THOUGHT THE shocked look on Fang's face was utterly priceless. It gave him the strength to do what he knew he had to do next.

Dylan rose into the air with powerful strokes, the air swirling and roiling around him. Fang had shot away from Dylan in shock, anger, and surprise, twisting his face into a grimace as his nose gushed from the blow. But Dylan matched him wing to wing. He was the hunter, his body strong and sure in the pursuit, his face set in grim expectation.

Dr. Williams had been right: He was stronger, more powerful, more advanced. He had been *created* for this.

There was only one way this could end.

In his mind's eye, Dylan saw the fight from above—a

giant bird of prey and a snarling, wounded grizzly clawing and screeching at each other, streaking violently through the sky like a shooting star, both intent on one thing: blood.

Dylan watched as the bear twisted his lean body defensively, his dark, matted hair lifted by the wind. He watched the paw swing and find its mark, saw blood gushing from fresh wounds. Then Dylan was aware of a spark of electricity, a wetness vibrating on his arm.

He saw those famous fangs, bared and gnashing as a deadly snarl built from somewhere vicious and animal within.

Then he watched the eagle, stalking its prey from above with graceful speed and huge breadth, wings spread, talons out, ready to strike.

Diving for the kill.

Going for the throat.

And before he could register what was going on, Max was there, between them, real and physical, her voice echoing in his eardrums.

"Dylan!" she wailed, blocking Fang, *cradling* him, propping his body up even as she kicked and clawed at Dylan's face. "If you ever loved me, if you care about me at all, *please*"—her voice broke as sobs overtook her, and it was like a knife slicing through him—"don't do this."

She was fighting him with all her strength, pulling at his hands, pleading with all her heart. Pleading for him to spare Fang's life.

As if waking from a nightmare, he blinked a few times and panted as he looked from the tears running down Max's dirty, bloody face to the hands clenched, viselike, around Fang's throat.

They were his hands, he understood with shock.

He had wanted to protect Max, he told himself miserably. But Fang's death, he realized, would kill her as surely as any whitecoat could.

That was when he realized he couldn't go through with it.

Dylan loved Max more than anything.

Even more than the survival of the earth.

69

JUST WHEN I thought Dylan was going to crush the life out of Fang forever, the word "us" changed everything.

You're better than this, Dylan, I had screamed at him. *They're the ones making you do this—not you. You don't want to kill Fang. Let him go. Do it for you. And me. Do it for us!*

When I was sure that Fang was on his last breath, when I was sure my heart was one second away from irreversibly shattering, Dylan suddenly released Fang's throat and shot away from us, his powerful wings beating so fast they were a blur.

I dropped to the ground with Fang's unconscious body in my arms, still weeping.

"Is Fang..." Nudge asked, her voice trembling.

I could only look at her solemnly as I heaved us both up

and staggered toward the house. I didn't know how to answer her yet, and I couldn't voice the fears snaking through my thoughts.

"Let's just get him inside," I said shakily.

With the flock close on my heels, I laid Fang on the couch, wondering if I would ever have furniture that wasn't bloodstained. Nudge hurried over with a blanket and carefully covered Fang. I looked at my flock, being so strong, and my throat threatened to close.

I sat down next to Fang and held his cold hand in mine, trying to warm it. I stroked his dark, bloodied hair. The blood vessels in his eyelids and cheeks had burst, and there were tiny red lines streaking over his pale face. The face I'd grown up with, the face I loved. His neck was all blotchy, covered in dark purple, hand-shaped bruises—it looked like Dylan was still choking him.

"He's supposed to be immortal, anyway, right?" Iggy said from next to me. He was trying to sound tough, but I heard the fear in his voice, and saw how tightly he was pressing his lips together. "*Right*, Max?"

I shook my head. Iggy hadn't quite understood Jeb's shorthand scientific gobbledygook, but I couldn't explain it to him now. I couldn't speak. All I could think about was what Angel had said long ago: *Fang will be the first to die.*

I pressed an ear to Fang's chest, holding my breath. His heartbeat was weak and erratic, but it was there.

"He's alive," I said with a sigh, sweet relief flooding through me. Behind me, Gazzy cheered, and I heard small, hiccupping sobs coming from Angel. "He's okay, he's okay—he's just knocked out," I continued, my voice hard and determined. "He's going to be *fine*." I concentrated on Fang, trying to will his strength back into him.

"Do you think he needs blood or x-rays or—" Iggy started to say, and then he suddenly froze, a strange expression on his face.

Everything changes now, I heard my Voice say in my head. *Be ready. You've won this battle, but the real threat has been unleashed. The war has only just begun.*

I watched Gazzy's face grow even paler and saw the despair in Nudge's eyes, and I realized that the Voice wasn't just in my own head this time. Every member of my little flock had heard the same thing.

Be ready, the Voice repeated. *The 99% Plan is in effect.*

70

I DIDN'T EVEN have time to launch into a full-fledged freak-out over the Voice's message before my thoughts were drowned out by a distinctive chopping sound that was quickly getting louder and louder.

"Is that a helicopter?" Nudge asked, peering out a window. "There's a helicopter now?"

The chopper was super close—almost right on our roof, it sounded like. I hated leaving Fang for even a second, but I hurried over to the window. Outside, the treetops were bent almost double and dead leaves were flying everywhere. The house windows were starting to shake when the whirring sound of the blades slowed and stopped.

"I seriously can't deal with this right now," I muttered. For the first time, I really didn't know if we were up to any new challenge. My flock was bloody and beaten up, Fang was still out cold, and Dylan was gone. If this was some new threat, I didn't have a Plan B. Or a Plan A, for that matter.

I needed a break. But leaders don't get breaks.

"Okay," I said, straightening my shoulders even though inside I was screaming. I pushed a strand of blood-soaked hair out of my eyes. "I'm going to go see what's up. If I'm not back in ten, I'm either dead or asleep on my feet. Stay with Fang—keep him safe. Do *not* come after me."

With that, I walked woodenly back outside. It was fully light out. I stepped over the fallen Erasers and past Jeb, who was still lying next to the porch, unconscious. I didn't have enough energy to feel anything toward the man who had created me, the man who had betrayed me in the worst way imaginable—more than once. I'd been awake since about three AM, and most of those hours had been spent locked in fatal combat. I was too exhausted to feel anything but despair.

The chopper had landed on a piece of flat ground right next to the house. I squinted but couldn't see through the tinted windows, so I stopped and waited to see what fresh disaster was about to emerge.

The chopper's small door opened.

I braced myself.

My mother, Valencia Martinez, stepped out.

That did it. My knees gave out, and I crumpled in an ungraceful pile on the trampled grass.

71

"MAX!" MY MOM cried, and her voice washed over me like a warm breeze. She sprinted toward me, her arms open, her face twisted with concern.

"It is really you?" I asked, blearily looking up at her as she lifted me from the ground. She nodded and smiled her warm, familiar smile.

After a quick embrace she pulled back and gently placed both of her hands on my shoulders, her worried eyes appraising my blood-spattered clothes and dirty face.

"Let me look at you," she said. "What happened to you?"

"Jeb," I said bleakly. "Jeb happened. And Ari. And his Erasers. And Dylan...He attacked Fang—they were *all* trying to kill Fang, and..." I couldn't stop the sobs that overtook me then.

"Oh, honey," she said, hugging me tight. "I'm so sorry. I tried to get here sooner...."

"It's not your fault," I said, still crying. I hugged her back with all I had, breathing in her warm, homey scent.

"I'm not so sure about that, Max," she said quietly, her voice wracked with pain.

I pulled away, wiping my nose on my dirty sleeve, and stared at her blankly. I couldn't process what she might have meant; I was too wrapped up in the joy of having her back.

Mom looked at me solemnly, seemingly prepared for the worst. "Where is Fang?" she asked. "Is he alive?"

I nodded, pointing toward the house, and she dashed off.

The next hour was a blur of my mom checking on Fang and then helping the rest of us get patched up as best we could. Gazzy and Nudge both needed stitches, and I was so glad that my mom was a trained medical professional. For animals, but still.

"Fang will be fine, I think," she said, and I breathed another sigh of relief. "He has a concussion, so he needs to take it easy for a while. But he should wake up soon. Everything else looks worse than it actually is."

I nodded. With Fang sorted out, I finally asked the other burning question that had been on my mind: "Mom, what happened to you? Where have you been all this time?"

Her eyes flicked to Angel and filled with something it took me a moment to recognize. "It's...a long story," she replied hesitantly. It was shame she had in her eyes, I realized. Angel blinked, looking down, and said nothing.

My heart froze as I remembered what she'd told me: *Max, your mom was there. I saw her. Dr. Martinez. She's one of them.* The expression on my mom's face now told me Angel hadn't been hallucinating.

"No," I said, drawing in a sharp breath. "No, Mom, not you..." I felt like I was trying to swallow a whole ice cube.

"Please believe me when I tell you this, Max," my mom said tentatively. "I was brainwashed. Jeb brainwashed me as effectively as the Doomsday Group did Ella and Iggy. You remember how quickly that cult spread, like a pandemic. I...I never thought I'd be a victim of that kind of thing, and it still seems impossible to me that it happened. I'm a doctor, a pragmatist, not some unhinged fanatic! It's a mystery that I'm going to investigate for the rest of my life. But, honestly, Max, I don't have time to deal with that just now. All I know is that I have to get you kids to safety right away—"

"Not so fast, Mom," I interrupted, crossing my arms over my chest and shaking my head in disbelief. "If you were brainwashed, how do I know you're not 'under the influence' anymore?"

She looked at me intently, her eyes pleading. "I know it's hard to believe, Max. But after Jeb left, this...spell, or whatever it is...disappeared. Wore off. I don't know. Jeb just knows me too well. He's an incredibly smart and powerful man, and apparently he's figured out how to use his power to control me. I somehow fell into believing again in a man I once thought could change the world, stupidly following him into the darkness."

For the first time, my mother seemed imperfect. And a hundred percent human.

"When Jeb left the lab," she rushed on, "I suddenly saw the true horror in everything and everyone around me at the facility. I knew Jeb was insane at that point. But I also gained valuable information as . . . one of them. I knew 99% was beginning, so I left the lab and immediately notified Pierpont that we had to get to you and the flock. To implement the final steps we'd been working on together for so long."

The rest of the flock was crowded around me, shocked into silence. My face was hard, giving nothing away as I listened. I didn't like the sound of the words "final steps we'd been working on together for so long." It seemed like this new development came with more secrets, more lies. The stuff my life was made of.

"I promise you this is the real me, Max." Mom swallowed, looking at me levelly. "And I promise you, all of you, that I'm back now. I know what's right, what's true, and I'm on your side."

None of us answered her or so much as breathed, but I could feel the eyes of each member of the flock on my face as they waited for my next move. Whatever I said, they would follow my lead.

"Angel, check her mind," I said faintly, still trying to

harden my heart against the possible outcome. "See if she's telling the truth."

My mom closed her eyes, openly accepting the mind reading. *Please let that be a good sign*, I said to myself.

After what seemed like multiple eternities, Angel said, slowly, "She's being honest. Dr. Martinez isn't with the 99% Plan anymore. She's a good guy."

72

"NINO HAS A jet waiting for us, back near the city," my mom said. "We can take the chopper there. With the 99% Plan taking effect and God knows how many scientists seeking Fang for his DNA, you won't be safe here. You need a new beginning."

Four pairs of eyes turned toward me, pleading. The flock waited for my decision.

"Yeah," I said wearily. "Getting out of here sounds good."

The flock responded with the biggest smiles I'd seen in weeks.

But as we raced through the house gathering our things, Total weaving between my legs, barking orders about packing techniques, two thoughts wouldn't leave my mind: *Where is Dylan?* And: *What about Jeb?*

I didn't know why Dylan had done what he'd done or where he'd disappeared to, so there was nothing I could do about the first question, regardless of how confused and devastated it made me feel. But Jeb *was* here, out in the Oregon air, unconscious, with broken ribs that *I'd* caused. If we left him, he would freeze during the night.

I was helping Angel and Nudge carry their bags to the chopper when I finally made my decision. I flagged down my mom, who was turning off the lights and shutting the front door. "Wait—we need to bring Jeb," I blurted before I could change my mind.

"*What?*" Angel hissed, recoiling in surprise.

Iggy was indignant. "Max, he wanted to *kill* Fang, we can't just—"

"We *can't* just leave him out there to die," I cut him off. "He saved our lives once, and we owe him this. No matter what he's done."

Sometimes being a leader isn't about winning. Sometimes it's about doing what's right, instead of what's powerful.

"We'll keep him under lock and key," my mom agreed, giving me a look that said *I'm proud of you.* "He's a sick man, but not an evil one."

She immediately set about tying up Jeb's hands and feet while the rest of us loaded Fang into to the chopper on a makeshift stretcher. Total had to be forcefully scooped and carried into the back, protesting all the while that he couldn't go anywhere that might be too far away from

Akila. Mom reassured Total that Akila would be waiting for him at the place we were headed. She refused to divulge anything further.

The pilot started the helicopter, and the deep noise of the blades filled our ears as we fastened our seat belts.

I sighed as the chopper lifted off the ground and we left everything—all of our emotional baggage, Ari, a hundred dead Erasers, and the empty house in Newton—behind us. I wondered briefly what the neighbors would think of the mess we'd left in our wake, and couldn't help smiling.

73

WE WERE FIVE hours into a very long flight on Nino Pierpont's fancy private jet when Fang's eyes finally fluttered open.

"Fang!" I shrieked. I was so ecstatic I almost kissed him right there, in front of everyone. Instead I settled for hugging him tightly, like my life depended on it—way too roughly for his injuries.

"Max?" he croaked. "What...happened?"

I took a deep breath and told Fang that he had been hurt really badly in a fight, and that when the fight was over, he was unconscious. I told him that Ari had been taken down in the fight, but I didn't mention Dylan. I told him how my mom had come for us, how it turned out that, in the end, Jeb was just another stupid whitecoat who had lost his mind. I was breathless, talking as fast as I could. I was afraid if I stopped talking, even for a second, I'd start sobbing again.

"Whoa, there." Fang smiled and reached up, tracing a hand down the side of my face, winding strands of my hair around his fingers. "Stop talking and let me just tell you how great it is to wake up staring at your face. Okay?"

That was maybe the most direct thing Fang had ever said to me. A lump formed in my throat. "Okay," I croaked.

"Okay, so...it's really great to wake up looking at your face." He blinked, like his eyes were still trying to focus. "It's...beautiful, actually."

The lump in my throat got bigger. Way bigger. "I thought..." I whispered, tears pricking my eyes. "I thought you were never going to wake up."

"Come on. You really thought I'd leave you right when things were getting interesting?" Fang gave a gruff little laugh that sounded more like a cough. "Not in a million years." His eyes turned serious then, and he took my hand, bringing it to his cracked, swollen lips. "I'll never leave you, Max. Not ever again."

My heart leaped. I squeezed his hand and nodded. "Me neither."

For the rest of the flight I didn't budge from Fang's side. Sometimes I just sat there and watched his bruised face as he slept. Sometimes I woke from my own dozing to see his dark eyes watching me, as if I were a stranger and he was meeting me for the first time. And the whole time, awake or asleep, Fang never let go of my hand. Not once.

And here's the weird thing: Even with all the awful stuff that had gone on, that was *still* going on, I felt content. I felt whole.

I felt *right*.

I wasn't afraid of anything anymore. With Fang and the flock by my side, I could face anything. Come what may.

"So, where are we going, again?" Fang asked, yawning. He squinted out the window.

"To the one place in the world where you'll be safe," my mom said, turning around in her plush seat a few rows ahead of us. "To paradise."

Book Four
PARADISE

74

SIX BIRD KIDS and one very jet-lagged flying dog stepped off Pierpont's plane into glorious sunshine and tropical humidity.

We left Jeb on the plane; my mom said that this place had a medical team who would deal with him, and that they knew to keep him under guard.

"Just a short walk to your new home," my mom said, and soon we were parading after her through the welcome shade of the rain forest.

I looked around me, struck dumb with wonder. Vines snaked up towering trees fuzzy with neon moss. Birds twittered and trilled all around us. Through a window of branches, we could see distant cliffs falling sharply to a beach of bleached sand and turquoise water.

My mom was right: If you looked up "paradise" in the dictionary, this would be it.

"Whoa," I breathed.

"To our new life," Fang said, threading his fingers in mine, his smile implying so many things we hadn't been able to put into words: Together. Our new life together.

I grinned, dizzy with the possibilities of this place.

"Oh, my gosh!" Nudge said breathlessly. "Iggy! Feel the moss on the trees. Everything is lush and gorgeous and *so* green. And there's parrots!" she squealed. "That's the noise you hear above, that weird cackle. There are tons of 'em—blue and red and yellow. They're huge!"

Gazzy flew up to join the parrots and started swinging from vines, Tarzan-style, and Iggy zoomed up after him, deftly maneuvering through the trees.

"Quickest way to ruin our first day in paradise? Scraping your feathered butts off the jungle floor!" Total yelled, and Gazzy hung upside down by one foot, giggling maniacally.

"Ooh, I bet there are waterfalls, too," Nudge continued, ignoring the boys. "Tropical paradises always have waterfalls! Don't they?"

My mom smiled indulgently. "They do, and there are."

"Tree house!" Gazzy yelled from above. "Oh, man! You guys, look at all the tree houses!"

The tree houses were camouflaged so well that I hadn't noticed them at first, but he was right—now I could see their shapes forming a village high in the jungle's canopy.

A village just for us.

"They have our names on the doors!" Gazzy yelled. "Nudge, this one's yours."

"Really?" Nudge bolted up there as fast as her wings would carry her.

Nudge's tree house was the most chic-looking of all the tree houses: ultramodern, with sleek, clean lines. It was minimal—almost delicate—and seemed to be held together by nothing more than sap. "A canopied bed!" I heard Nudge exclaim from inside. This was followed by a "Gazzy! Off!" I snorted with laughter.

"I think that's yours over there, Total," my mom said, pointing to an enormous mansion of a tree house.

"Mine?" Total asked, gaping upward. "Oh, Dr. M! Look at those glorious arches, the Grecian lines! Plush, with understated elegance and seaside charm," he gushed. "So classy! So regal! It's so ... me."

Just at that moment we heard a bark—and it wasn't Total's high-pitched yap, but the joyful call of a much bigger canine. A wet nose peeked out from between some of the tree-house branches above.

"*Akila!*" Total was off in a flash to be reunited with his furry lady love.

Wow. They really have thought of everything, I thought.

Laughing, Angel, Fang, and I followed my mom farther down the path.

"This is you, Max." My mom nodded up at a mammoth banyan tree.

My new home was almost impossible to see if you didn't know it was there—the perfect hideout. At the top of the towering trunk, a canopy of leaves reached for the sun.

"It's beautiful," I said in awe.

"It suits you," Fang said from behind me, his breath making the hairs on my neck stand up.

I looked at the brittle, gnarled roots snaking all the way up and around the trunk, creating a hard, protective layer for the tree's core. Maybe Fang wasn't so far off.

"How do we get in?" I asked.

My mom turned and smiled at me. "You fly."

75

I COULD FLY in here, I thought breathlessly. *Inside my own house.*

The tree was completely hollow. The ceiling was made of thick protective glass, but it was all the way up top, near the banyan's broad, glossy leaves. Strips of sunlight filtered through the canopy, reminding me of old, dusty churches with swallows darting among the rafters.

Angel stayed with me to explore the place after Mom had taken Fang somewhere—who knows where; maybe a floating tree-house hospital in paradise?—to remove the bandages from his quickly healing wounds. As we explored, all kinds of cool little details caught our eyes. The furniture looked like the tree itself had just grown naturally into rough, chairlike shapes, and tunnels from the main room led to elaborate balconies with comfy hammocks. It all looked kind of haphazard, but at the same time beautifully, thoughtfully designed.

Someone knows me very *well*, I thought.

I pressed a button on one wall and a metal ladder spiraled silently down to the jungle floor below. Mechanical. *Fancy.*

I soared upward, the wood circling around me in a blur, and found the latch to a door in the glass ceiling that lead to the roof. There was a small balcony high above the jungle's canopy where I could see everything: the towering cliffs on the other side of the island, the sea lapping against the sandy coast…and, of course, it was an ideal spot for spying on my wayward flock.

The perfect perch. Angel and I sat there together for a moment.

I was dreaming of long days of swimming, cliff-diving, soaring above the most beautiful place I'd ever seen, so I was surprised to suddenly catch sight of Angel's distant, unsettling look.

"What, honey?" I said gently.

She looked up at me urgently. "I want to stay here forever," she said, gripping my hand tightly. "Max, I never want to leave."

"You won't have to, sweetie," I promised her. I peered at the banyan's sturdy silhouette and beamed. "None of us will ever have to leave again."

I felt so much relief as I said it, knowing it was true. But

Angel was still staring at me, like she didn't want to let me out of her newly recovered sight. Her eyes were huge in her little face, and she seemed pretty spooked.

"Angel?" I said uneasily. "Are you sure you're okay?"

"Yeah," she said, but it came out as a stressed little squeak. "It's just…nothing."

I put my arm around her. "I know you've been through a lot lately, but that's all over now. You can trust my mom. We're thousands of miles from anyone who would hurt you, and totally off the radar. It's safe here. Really."

Angel let out her tense breath and smiled. "Thanks, Max." She walked over to the doorway. "I'll be at my tree house if you want to find me."

As I gave Angel a quick good-bye hug, I noticed that a thick branch connected my home to another tree house. I shimmied across it, wondering which member of the flock's butt I'd have to kick in the mornings, weighing the pros and cons of waking up to Nudge's sugary pop music versus being downwind of Gazzy's infamous morning emissions.

Instead, the bold, black letters staring back at me from the wooden plaque on the door caused a helpless little squeak to come out of my mouth: DYLAN.

Does. Not. Compute.

That name on the door was like a hard fist to my stomach, and I felt all the stuff I'd been so good at swallowing come back up: Anger that he'd almost killed Fang in front of all of us. Hurt and confusion over his complete freakout. Shame for all the stupid, fluttery feelings I'd felt when he looked at me with those ocean eyes of his. Clearly he was *not* my perfect other half. Everything came spewing out like some sort of emotional vomit.

Romantic, huh?

And because the universe just loves to screw with my emotions, I felt a hand on my shoulder right then, and I nearly jumped out of my skin. Was he...?

"Don't worry, Max," my mom said, striding past me.

I exhaled. The ladder—I'd left it down.

With one hard wrench, she pried the nameplate off the door and tossed it out of the tree like yesterday's garbage. "That sign will be replaced." Mom sighed.

"Uhhh," I groaned, totally incapable of any other response. I clenched my jaw and concentrated on pushing every stupid thought of Dylan back down again.

"Fang! Up here! Come see your house," Mom called from the balcony. She looked back at me with...what? Pity? "I'm sorry, honey," she said, giving my arm a squeeze. "He wasn't...expected."

76

"THERE'S SOMETHING ELSE you need to know," my mom said when we all met up again, and Fang's eyes flicked to mine.

Was it all too good to be true?

"What?" I asked uneasily.

"Let me show you," she said, and then she called the rest of the flock to join her.

After a short, brisk hike through the jungle, during which my anxiety steadily grew, the flock finally emerged to face the spectacular cliffs we'd seen from our houses. My heart leaped. I couldn't wait to dive over the edge and weave through all those crazy crevices, the wind surging through my feathers.

But before I could take off, my mom put two fingers to

her mouth and let out a crisp, high-pitched whistle. A signal. The flock looked around, confused. The place seemed abandoned.

Then slowly, tentatively, people started emerging from the surrounding trees and from fractures in the rocks. I remembered what Angel had said about my mom earlier, that she was a traitor, and had a moment of panic. *Hostiles?*

I immediately took a defensive stance and the flock followed suit, ready to attack, but then I realized something.

"There aren't any adults," I said, relaxing. "It's all kids."

Their expressions were serene, welcoming, and as they came closer I saw scales, tails, metal arms.

"They're mutants!" Gazzy squeezed Iggy's arm.

"Yes," my mother answered. "All *enhanced* kids. Just like you."

As if to punctuate her words, a girl who looked about eight years old unfurled a pair of speckled black and gray wings, laughing to her friends. They all soared upward ten, twenty, thirty feet.

"Just like us," Nudge whispered, echoing my mom.

Even Fang was grinning. It was impossible not to. After so many years of being experimented on, of doing what everyone else wanted us to do, of running, running, running, we were finally in a place where we belonged.

"Max," Mom said, and I followed her gaze to the jungle behind us.

There, with a ginormous grin on her face, was my half sister.

"Ella!" I squealed as she barreled into me for a bear hug. I hadn't seen her since our mom had her rescued and squirreled away from the 99% cult, who almost had her brainwashed. Back before Angel disappeared.

In the middle of our embrace, someone tapped on Ella's shoulder and she turned around to see Iggy, looking shy and totally lovestruck. Her face lit up in a huge grin and she leaned in and kissed him, right there in front of all of us, and then Iggy wrapped her up in a long, tender hug.

Watching them, I was drunk with love and hope and happiness all at once, and as the other mutant kids on the cliffs started cheering, I looked at Fang standing beside me, silent and strong. His fingers found their way to mine and his smile said everything I couldn't.

We were finally, truly home.

77

THEN THE PARTY started.

We walked into a hidden cove with lush green foliage surrounding a breathtaking waterfall, just like my mom had promised. I was waiting for unicorns to come galloping out and fairies to start singing.

Nudge waded into the water, grinning as two girls her age chatted her up, their wings unfurled proudly around them. She looked so happy, so comfortable in her own skin.

Iggy did a perfectly executed back dive with a half twist off the cliff, slicing the shallow water next to Ella with minimal splash, and I thought she was going to faint right there.

Even Angel was looking more like her former self,

laughing and splashing with Total and Akila as the Gasman torpedoed into them underwater.

Fang and I were seated with Mom and Nino Pierpont at a wooden table off to the side, watching the festivities. Pierpont looked impossibly cool in his deliberately rugged, undoubtedly expensive trekking outfit as he watched us wolf down a huge meal of braised pork and paella, prepared by his bustling team of private chefs. If there is a way to our hearts, it is definitely though our stomachs—which is why I was getting a little nervous.

"So, what's the catch?" Fang asked, obviously thinking the same thing.

I housed a giant bite of sausage, wanting desperately for there not to be a catch, for once.

"Hmm?" Mom asked, too innocently.

"Like, is this how it all ends?" I asked. "No more experiments? No more running? Happily ever after, sleeping under the stars in our beautiful tree houses, living carefree in our island paradise?"

My mom smiled, but her eyes said something different.

"I wish, Max...I hope. God, I hope." Her glance flicked to Pierpont, who was shifting uncomfortably in his seat. "But..."

"But what?" Fang asked accusingly, tensing beside me.

"This is your new world. Your new community," my mom said. "But it's a community for..."

"The ones who will survive," Pierpont finished her sentence gravely.

"Wait," Fang said, dropping his fork. "The ones who *what*?"

I looked at my mom in alarm, and she nodded sadly. I'd been hearing about the world ending for so long, had been preparing for this moment for years, but it still hit me like a rock falling out of the sky. "Can someone tell us what's going on?" I asked, my voice rising. "Can someone, for once, please just be *honest* with us?"

"Where do I even start?" My mom sighed.

"How about with the part we know—that the 99 Percenters want to save the earth and its environment through the genocide of... well, almost the entire human race. So, what exactly is their plan?"

My mom took a deep breath. I knew this was going to be hard to listen to, and I took Fang's hand.

"They've been working for years on developing a form of avian flu that has a terrifying ability to quickly mutate and has been manufactured to mimic other, even deadlier, viruses, ebola among them." Mom looked me in the eye, letting her words sink in. "The virus is called H8E, but it's known among the 99 Percenters as 'The Finisher.'"

"So we're more susceptible to it because we're bird kids?" I asked.

"No, actually," Mom said, smiling. "It seems counterintuitive, but because of your mixed DNA, you kids have a natural immunity to it that we haven't seen in any other species. Of course, Ella and Nino and I, and some of the other enhanced kids—and Jeb, of course—aren't immune."

My heart jumped into my throat.

"And if, by some fluke and despite our precautions, the virus spread to this island and we became infected, and the virus then mutated after evolving through the simple human system—"

"You don't have to worry about that, Maximum," Pierpont cut in, waving at my mom to shut up. I narrowed my eyes at him. "We've been working for years—since before you were born—to create a safe refuge for those who have the most hope of surviving and continuing the human race. We believe that you children will absolutely thrive here."

"Wow, and here I would've thought that if you knew a biotoxin was being manufactured for decades, you might've been spending that time trying to create a vaccine or something," I said dryly.

Pierpont took off his chic safari hat and ran his hands through his short, silvery hair.

"It mutates too fast for that, Max," my mom said, unfazed as usual by my insolent audacity.

"On the surface, of course, you have a tropical paradise," Pierpont continued, gesturing widely at the waterfall. "But should the worst occur, you will be safe inside a luxurious city of caves protected by a force field created with the latest technology. A complex system of passages will allow you to live quite comfortably belowground."

"You mean until the biotoxin becomes extinct, along with the rest of the human race?" Fang asked.

Mom and Pierpont were quiet, which I took as a "yes."

"So...what exactly does this ultimate toxin do?" I asked, not sure if I really wanted to know. But I had to find out. I didn't want any more secrets.

My mom studied her notebook. Then her eyes flicked to Ella, who was splashing in the waterfall. Then she stared down at her shoes. Mom was one tough cookie. If she couldn't say it outright, it was way worse than I'd thought.

"Just give it to us straight," I said, huddling closer to Fang, who wrapped his arm around my shoulders. "We can handle it."

"Okay." She sighed and started to read. "The toxin is first inhaled and moves through the lungs, causing a slight cough and, in some cases, a rash. The cells multiply, creating internal fissures in the organs and hemorrhaging into the bloodstream. A short time later, boils appear on the skin's surface. When the boils burst, the wounds weep, shedding billions of the highly contagious cells and infecting, basically, anyone in the vicinity." Mom cleared her throat. "At this point, with so many open sores secreting contagion, the victim will likely develop a staph infection that will quickly progress to necrotizing fasciitis, literally rotting the skin off the body in a matter of days."

So, to break it down: You breathe in this little villain, and it basically liquefies your organs, then moves to your bloodstream, and then rots off the surface of your skin until you're a bleeding, writhing mass of agony, all while infecting everyone around you in every way possible.

I felt bile rising in my throat. Fang's face had gone white, and I could feel him shivering. "Mark," he said under his breath. "The contagion..."

We were remembering the same thing: Mark's last words at the hospital where Angel had been held captive. "Mom," I said, "could the...threat have been released already?"

My mother didn't flinch. She obviously knew the answer. And she was going to tell it to me straight.

"Yes," my mom said softly. "The toxin itself will kill almost all of the population on its own. But based on the agonizing effects it has on the human body, we estimate that at least half of the deaths will be from suicide."

I let out a slow, unsteady breath.

It was so much worse than I could've imagined.

78

LATER THAT NIGHT—after I'd finally been able to put all of what I'd learned out of my mind for a few blessedly peaceful moments—Fang crept across the branch connecting our tree houses.

He gave a low whistle. "Penthouse, eh?"

"Yeah." I nodded, watching the lithe movements of Fang's body as he surveyed my new digs, his glossy black wings folded behind him. "Honeymoon suite."

Fang turned around and cocked an eyebrow, and my stomach leaped. "Well, in that case..." He strode toward me and, in one slick move, picked me up. He carried me out to a giant hammock on one of the balconies. I think we've established that I'm not the type of girl who needs to actually be swept off her feet, but the suggestion in his mischievous eyes was enough to make even the most cynical assassin woozy.

We settled in together, and I was incredibly aware of the heat coming from Fang's body, which was pressed against mine as we snuggled.

He nuzzled my neck, inhaling deeply. "Mmm. You smell so good."

"Oh, yeah," I said, smirking. "I call this new perfume 'Le Jungle grime et tropical BO.'"

"Dirt and sweat. *Very* sexy."

I laughed, but Fang's voice was husky, and he was already leaning closer. Then his soft lips were on mine.

Everything in my body was buzzing, aching for more, but there was a kernel of guilt buried underneath it that I just couldn't ignore.

"Fang," I whispered.

"Mmm?" Fang mumbled, his lips brushing my neck and sending shivers through me.

I kissed him again. Lately, my life felt like a freaking rags-to-riches fairy tale, complete with the perfect guy whispering sweet nothings in my ear. This felt so easy. So right. So *overdue*. Everything was finally as it should be. Except…

The flip side of that was that while we were here, in paradise, chosen to be saved, humanity was about to be wiped out. It was so completely screwed up.

I sighed, pulling away from Fang's embrace. "I'm sorry. I just keep thinking about what my mom said. Trying to make sense of it."

"I know," Fang said softly, brushing my knotted hair out of my eyes. "I was trying not to think about it, pretend it wasn't happening, but it's always there now, isn't it? I keep thinking of my blog, all those kids reading it, dying in the way that Dr. M. described. It's, like, totally...incomprehensible." I couldn't tell if it was him or me who was trembling.

I was so frustrated I wanted to scream. "We've been searching for something like this forever—safety, a place that could finally, really be home. And now that we have it, it's at the expense of everyone else's survival."

"Welcome to the real world," Fang said, bitterness creeping into his voice. "Where kids are raised in cages, six-year-olds are tortured for the 'betterment of science'"— we both stiffened, thinking of Angel—"and a group of genocidal wackjobs can wipe out the entire planet with a bug cooked up in someone's kitchen."

Fang and I were silent for a long time, the trees casting shadows on our faces and the knowledge of the world's imminent doom sitting like the Grand Canyon between us. The moon shone down on us, a giant eye, a quiet witness.

I thought back to those miserable early days in the cages at the School and the short-lived freedom afterward, when Fang just felt like a brother and Jeb actually felt like a father. When I barely knew how to survive, let alone fight. When I first heard my Voice telling me I had to save the world.

How long ago those days felt now.

"I just feel so, so old now," I said, looking up through the leaves at the sky with its endless stars. "Like...twenty-one or something."

Fang snickered. "We could always create a new birthday for ourselves," he said, reminding me that we'd done that once.

"Seriously. How ridiculous is it that we can't legally drink alcohol, but the fate of the whole freaking world is on our shoulders?"

Fang shifted in the hammock so he could peer down at my face in the moonlight, a wry half smile on his lips. "Since when do you care about what's legal?" I jabbed him in the ribs. Then his gravelly voice turned serious again, and I felt like he was looking right into me. "Also, saving the world isn't on us anymore, Max," Fang said. "Or you. We're past that."

I blinked up at him and felt the last three years of my life fall away in shreds.

He was right, of course. But if I wasn't supposed to save the world...

Then who is Maximum Ride?

79

FANG WRAPPED HIS strong, sinewy arms around me. He stroked the spot between my wings as we swayed in the hammock in the cool night air. My whole body screamed to just drown in this moment with Fang, in his love—one hundred percent mine now, *finally*—but my conscience just wouldn't shut up.

"I know I should be grateful," I said after a few moments, my mind whirring. "But to be honest, I kind of resent Nino Pierpont—and even my mom—for protecting us, for saving only us. Like just because others don't have wings or aren't enhanced they're not superior enough to live?"

"It's so frustrating," Fang said, sighing. "We've spent our whole lives either being totally exploited or trying to protect other people. And this time, there's no way to save them, no one to kill."

"We're powerless." I sighed. We're all aware of my control issues.

"It kills me," he agreed. "But I *do* know that we were brought here, that we were saved, so that you could help this island full of kids who need you. You're one of the most stubborn people I've ever met, Maximum Ride. You're also incredibly intelligent, and beautiful, and charming when you want to be, which is probably why you can manipulate people into doing what you want most of the time."

"I'm not manip—" I protested.

"But those qualities also make you a brilliant leader," Fang interrupted. "And an awesome fighter. That's why you were chosen for this—to lead the new generation."

"And meanwhile the rest of the world's just screwed?" I said.

"Maybe." His soft feathers brushed against my skin, enveloping us. "But if the world's doomed either way, maybe we can have this *one* night of our lives to just be together and forget that anyone else exists. To just be happy."

I was quiet for a moment. *Just be happy.* How I ached for that freedom.

"Max?"

"Hmm?"

Fang lifted my chin and looked down at me intently.

He took a deep breath. "I've waited my whole life to be with you. Do you get that?"

My heart fluttered as I nodded. I did. I felt exactly the same way.

"So can't we just enjoy this? Just for a little while?"

Fang's eyes were liquid black in the darkness, that familiar lopsided little smile playing across his lips. His lips... My heart raced as he leaned in again, never taking his eyes from my face. Then those perfect lips met mine in the softest, most tender kiss, and I closed my eyes and breathed in the sweetness of him.

When I finally opened my eyes again, dazed with happiness, Fang looked shocked, almost pained, like he'd just realized something.

"What?" I asked, nervous.

"Nothing. I just..." His voice was hoarse. "This is *everything*. You're all I need."

Then Fang's lips crashed into mine again, even more passionately, almost desperately. I kissed him back fiercely. I felt his fingers tangle in my hair, then his hands moving over my stomach, my hips, pulling me closer.

I pressed against him, our legs twisted in the hammock. My entire body was shaking as I kissed him deeper, with a desire—a *need*—I didn't even know I had. I wasn't actually positive I was even breathing.

Fang held me tightly, like he'd never, ever let go again, and we kissed for what felt like an eternity, for all of those tense moments that had been building between us for years, and for every second we'd been apart. We kissed like we were inhaling each other, like we would live and die in this moment.

We kissed like the world was ending.

80

AND THEN, SUDDENLY, it was like the world really *was* ending.

Without warning, an explosion tore through my tree house, dangerously rocking the structure like an earthquake. Adrenaline overloaded my system and Fang and I scrambled to untwist from the hammock and ran inside. Our senses were hammered from all sides: Glass shattering. Wood splintering. Someone crashing toward us with the force of a tornado. *What on earth—*

"GET OUT!" someone yelled at full volume. "GET OUT *NOW!*"

A tall figure emerged from the shadows, looking totally strung out and insane and desperate.

I nearly shrieked in fury. After ruining everything else, now he was ruining my perfect night with Fang.

"Dylan!" I exploded at him. "What are you even *doing* here? On *our* island?"

"Max! Just give me a chance to explain—"

"A chance?" My mouth hung open. I could not believe what I was hearing. "How *dare* you. You went ballistic!" I yelled. "You abandoned the flock. And, *oh, yeah*, you TRIED TO KILL FANG! You don't get anything, do you? There are *no more chances!*"

"But this is it!" Dylan persisted. "I *saw* something, in the sky." His eyes were wild. "We have to get out right now!"

"No. *You* need to get out," Fang said in a low voice. He stepped closer so that his face was inches from Dylan's. "Now."

Dylan didn't flinch, but grabbed my wrist and tried to pull me toward the door. Fang shot forward, batting his hand away. Fang's face was warped with anger, his body rigid and his wings spread wide. He looked deadly.

Things were spiraling out of control.

"Look, I know things haven't been the best between us lately," Dylan said, backtracking. "But you guys just have to trust me—"

"Trust you?" Fang almost spit. "Why should we trust you?"

"Because I have always, always had Max's best interests at heart," Dylan answered. Fang scoffed, but Dylan continued, his voice rising. "Because every second you stay here you're putting her at risk—putting everyone at risk. Do you really want that on your shoulders? Don't you care about her at all?"

"Enough!" I yelled, stepping between them. "Okay," I snapped, pointing to Dylan. "You have sixty seconds. Start talking. Now."

Dylan swallowed. "I saw something. In the sky," he said, breathing heavily, trying to speak coherently. "I don't know how to explain. We have to get to the caves, get all the kids out. Now."

I shook my head. "It's okay. We know about the plague and the 99% Plan. This place was built to protect us. We're safe."

"Even if no one else is," Fang muttered from behind me.

"None of that matters!" Dylan shrieked. His eyes were wild, crazed. He looked like he was about to jump out of his skin. "This isn't a plague. Not even close."

I put a hand on his arm to try to calm him. After everything we'd been through, it still hurt to see him like this. "You...saw something in the sky," I said gently, trying to make sense of what he was saying. "Did it have wings? Was it a jet? A flyboy?"

"No, nothing like that." Dylan shook his head. "It's something...big. And it's moving too fast for me to clearly see what it is. But it's headed this way."

Fang walked to the window and peered out. I looked at him questioningly, but he shook his head. "Sky's totally clear. The leaves are still—there's not even any wind. Are you sure you didn't just see a shooting star, buddy?" Fang asked dryly.

Dylan's eyes hardened, his jaw tightening. "It was no everyday shooting star."

I crossed my arms over my chest, thinking.

I glanced back at Fang and saw his eyes flashing threateningly through his curtain of dark hair. He was rational to a fault. My *real* "other half."

And then there was Dylan, in front of me, looking all broken and insane and like he really needed me.

"Do you not hear what I'm telling you?" Dylan asked in frustration. "Max, I was created to protect you."

"Protect *me*?" I bristled. "I have spent years leading this flock, making split-second decisions based on well-honed instincts," I growled. "You have been alive for, what, a minute? And you've spent the past few days having a well-documented meltdown. Now, after almost murdering Fang, you have the nerve to show up here, to insist that we follow you because something weird is about to just...fall from the sky?" I was hitting a fever pitch. "Who do you think needs protection more, Dylan, me or you?"

His eyes were pleading, but I wasn't moving. "It's coming *now*," he said. "Please."

I sighed. "Dylan, just...go."

"Fine, stay here. I'm getting the rest of the kids to the caves. I'm not having their deaths on my head." Dylan sighed sadly. "I know you don't trust me anymore, Max.

But I've never lied to you, not once, and though it might seem like I've done some questionable things, I'm not crazy. You have to know that everything I've ever done, I did for you."

I cringed as he turned his back on us, his shoes crunching over the broken glass.

"And Max," Dylan called from the doorway, "after I get everyone to safety, I'll be back for you. Even if it means dying with you out here. That's the only way I want my life to end. With you."

81

"WHO DOES THAT guy think he is?" Fang exploded after Dylan was out of sight.

"Seriously!" I was as cranky as a wet cat and pacing furiously. "What the heck does he think he's doing barging into my house"—I gestured dramatically—"in the middle of—" I locked eyes with Fang. He raised an eyebrow, and his smirk sent a buzz through my whole body. "In the middle of the night. Trying to freak everyone out?"

I yanked an upturned table back over and slammed the door Dylan had left open.

"Max," Fang said cautiously. When I turned around, there was uncertainty on his face. "Do you think he might've really seen something? His vision is crazy sharp, isn't it?"

"Oh, please," I huffed. "It's not that great. And I don't know if he's short-circuiting or what, but he's clearly not the brightest bulb right now."

Fang nodded and bent to right an overturned chair. One of the reasons Fang and I work so well together? He keeps his mouth shut when I'm in fire-breathing dragon mode. Unlike Blondie down there.

At that point, I'd almost gotten used to Dylan strapping us in for his own personal roller-coaster ride of highs and lows, complete with lingering nausea at the whole rotten experience. This, however, was on a whole new level.

I was made to protect you, he'd said, his sea-blue eyes begging me to trust him, still full of that same fierce drive he'd shown when I'd taught him to fly, not so very long ago. But that dopey innocence, which had seemed almost endearing then, was nowhere in sight now.

I shook my head. I couldn't afford to be sentimental. Not anymore. Sentimentality is for suckers. And a sucker, I ain't.

Harden your heart.

Done. My heart is a freaking diamond. Only less glittery.

I bent to help Fang pick up the pieces of glass from the shattered window, and I couldn't help staring down at the havoc Dylan was already wreaking on our little paradise. The place had gone from zero to sixty in minutes, and I watched as he herded dozens of hysterical kids into the ultra-secure underground cave system.

Abuse of privileges. Mom was gonna freak.

"Gazzy!" I shouted when I spotted him moving along in his bobbing gait. "Nudge!" Iggy was with them, consoling Ella as they hurried toward the caves. Even Total was barking anxious orders at Akila in their dog language. "You guys, he's delusional. Cuckoo. There's nothing to worry about!"

In the chaos, they didn't seem to hear me.

"Oh, no," I fumed. "This. Will. Not. Stand." Making a mess was one thing. Hijacking my flock was another. "Wait, where's—"

"Angel." Fang pointed at the ragged-looking ball of feathery fluff zooming toward us through the trees.

She was sobbing as she crashed into my arms.

"Whoa," I said, cuddling her close. "It's okay, Ange. You're okay."

Angel shook her head, her soft curls framing her tear-streaked face.

"You guys have to get to the caves," she said, hiccupping. "It's coming. Dylan saw—"

"Yeah, I'm going to put a stop to that," I reassured her.

"No!" she wailed, her blue eyes wide with fear. "Dylan knows what he's doing. I saw things when I was in that lab, Max. Horrible things." Her little face contorted, and my mother-bear instincts raged. *As soon as we get off this island,* I swore, *I am going to hunt down those sickos who hurt my baby.*

"But we're never going to leave here, Max. We can't leave. You promised!" Angel cried, reading my mind.

I wiped the tears from her face and cupped her tiny chin in my hands. "It's okay, sweetie. Deep breaths. What did you see in the lab?"

"I saw trees falling over like dominoes. This place, coated in ash. The light comes first, then the sound. And you and Fang, blown out of the sky." Fang's dark eyes flicked to my face, but he didn't move. "When we landed, it seemed familiar, but I wasn't sure. It all makes sense now, though. Dylan is right—the sky is falling."

It's time, the Voice inside my head said. *Listen to her, Max.*

82

THE WORLD WAS ending, and we were in paradise.

I knew I should join the others, kiss away the rest of humanity, and spend the next fifty years snuggled up to my winged prince charming, finally free.

Fang and Angel were both studying my face closely. I shook my head slowly. I knew this was the decision that would define my life.

I just didn't have it in me to die like a coward.

"I'm flying back to the States," I said. "Now." I stepped past them, out onto the limb between the tree houses. Below, the jungle was quiet, the leaves rustling softly. Except for a few small figures I could see at the cliffs in the distance, everyone was already safe in the caves. If I was going to do this, if I was going to walk away from my flock, maybe forever, I had to go before I lost my nerve.

"What?" Angel looked horrified.

"Are you sure?" Fang asked, his face trusting and true.

I nodded, trying not to look into his eyes, trying not to think about what I was leaving behind. "If the toxin has been engineered like my mom said, there has to be an antidote. Or maybe Mark was lying. Maybe the contagion hasn't been released. Maybe we can stop the psychopaths before they release the bug. But if it *is* released...Well, at least we can warn people."

Angel shook her head. "Max, you don't understand what you're up against."

"Look, it's not like the odds haven't been stacked against me before," I said, trying to sound reassuring. "I always come out all right in the end, don't I?" I didn't say what everyone else was thinking: that it might actually *be* the end this time.

"Please don't do this now," Angel pleaded, reaching for my arm. "We have to get to the caves. Fang, tell her! We'll be safe, I promise. Just come with us."

Listen to her, the Voice repeated. *Go.*

I'd been obeying my Voice for so long, trusting whatever it said, even when it seemed to be mocking my existence. But I couldn't do it this time. Not when the consequences were so major.

"I can't, sweetie," I said to Angel. "I'm tired of running from the unknown. If this threat is real, I'm going to face it, whatever it is, with the rest of the world." I looked at Fang, standing next to her. *I'm sorry*, I mouthed, my heart breaking.

But Fang walked out to the limb and took my hand. He brought it to his lips and, without taking his smoldering, coal-black eyes from my face, said, "I'm with Max."

"Fang, no, you can't," I said. If this really was it, the end of the world, I couldn't ask this of him.

"Yes, I can. We'll fly back to face 99%," he said, nodding at me.

I stared at Fang for a long moment. It felt like we were one person.

"I'm with you," he repeated solemnly.

"But it's not them!" Angel shrieked from the ledge. "Aren't you listening? All the preparation Dr. Martinez and Pierpont and Jeb and all the other whitecoats did, poking and prodding and testing us, shooting us up with God knows what to make us immune—it was all totally point- less! It's not coming from 99%. It's coming from the sky."

Fang shrugged. "Then we'll face the thing in the sky. Whatever it is, we'll face it together." He gave my hand a squeeze, and tears streamed down my face.

"You'll die here!" Angel cried. "You'll both die, falling, just like what I saw."

I looked down at her, not sure how to explain myself. "Angel, I was supposed to save the world," I said quietly. I paused for a moment, realizing the gravity of that state- ment, and then stood up straighter, suddenly more sure of myself than I'd ever been. "I was supposed to save the whole world—not just the 'special' ones, not just the ones who have the protection of some multibillionaire. So if the rest of the world has to die, I have to go down with them."

I looked out across the row of abandoned tree houses with the pristine beaches in the background.

So long, paradise. It was nice knowing you.

Fang and I snapped out our wings and prepared for takeoff.

"Max!" Angel shouted. "Listen to me. You have to. I'm your Voice!"

83

I COULDN'T HELP but gasp. Then I quickly regrouped. I retracted my wings and shot her a supremely annoyed look. "You're not serious," I managed to say.

"You always listen to your Voice, right?" Angel said, hovering in front of us, her white wings outspread. "So please, please, listen this time."

"Are you really going to do this right now?" I growled. "Come on. I think we've all grown out of playing games at this point, Angel. You especially."

"I'm not playing games. It's me. It always has been."

"Let's just go, Max," Fang said, his fingers brushing mine. "You know what she's doing."

"I've always been your Voice," Angel insisted. I'm sure my face positively dripped with skepticism—I'm not exactly good at hiding such things—but she started counting on her fingers. "Before you found your mom, way back when we were looking for the Institute, your Voice guided you into the sewers with a riddle, right? Something about rainbows?" She cocked an eyebrow.

There's a pot of gold under every rainbow, Max.

Angel laughed, and it sounded creepy, almost disembodied. "I definitely had more fun with it, in the beginning, being inside your head." Her eyes darkened, and I looked at Fang uneasily. "Then it got more serious. When you first killed Ari, the Voice told you that you had to do it, didn't it?"

I winced, thinking of the day I'd murdered my half brother. The first time, when he had really felt like family. I was speechless. We didn't talk about that day.

Why was she doing this?

"That was me, too. I could feel your anguish, Max. And I knew he'd come back anyway, again and again, worse every time."

"Angel." Fang's voice was hard, protective. "That's enough."

But she went on.

"I was the one who told you that you had a greater mission in the first place. This is that mission: leading the new society after the apocalypse."

The Voice had said all of those things, true. And, true, no one knew about them but me. But Angel could read minds. Of course she could know everything the Voice had ever said to me. She was manipulating me.

Again.

"No, Angel. The only thing *you* told me was that Fang was going to die." I looked at her accusingly.

"I told you that Fang would be the first to die because I saw it, in a vision. I saw him falling."

"And you were wrong about that, weren't you?" I asked. "He's still here."

"It's still true, though." Angel frowned. "It's not over yet. Soon, but not yet."

No. NO. I shook my head against her idiotic claims, her attempts at mind control. We had been through all of this too many times before.

"I know it hurts," Angel said sadly. "Didn't I tell you to harden your heart?"

"You're wrong," I said through tears, clutching Fang's hand. "You're lying."

"I told you knowledge was a terrible burden, Max," Angel whispered, and I could hear the Voice saying those exact words in my head, years before. "That's why I couldn't tell you. Do you know how hard it is, seeing everything that's going to happen all the time?" There were tears shimmering in her eyes, a bitterness in her voice. She sounded jaded, old. So much older than a seven-year-old should ever sound.

"Imagine feeling what people feel, thinking what they think. It's so hard to stop listening, even when it hurts. Your Voice said she considered you a friend and loved you more than anyone. I meant it, Max. I always will. Don't you trust me?"

I thought about that question long and hard.

How I'd missed her, how I'd felt like my heart had been ripped out of my chest when we thought she was dead. But it was Angel who tried to hijack my leadership, who put the flock in danger over and over again. Angel who could kill us all.

She was my baby, and I loved her so, so much. But did I trust her?

Angel's face crumpled; she looked hurt and betrayed. She turned from us then and soared off toward the cliffs.

Don't deny the truth, the Voice said inside my head, and this time it was Angel's voice, sweet and coaxing. *Now is your time! Save yourself and the others! Do it now!*

I spun around, flabbergasted. I was choking on tears.

"What are we supposed to do?" I asked Fang. I'd been doing this for so long, taking on the responsibility, making all the decisions, that I'd forgotten what it felt like to have absolutely no clue where to turn. "After all that, what the heck are we supposed to do now?"

Fang shook his head and stroked the sides of my face with his slender fingers.

"I've spent my life trying to deny what I felt, when all I ever really wanted was to be with you, Max," he said. "I don't care what Angel says. I'm with you. Always. Whatever you decide."

But as I looked into Fang's angular face, his pupils suddenly dilated to pinheads as the world lit up around us.

I wasn't going to get to decide, after all.

84

THE SKY WAS on fire.

I mean really, actually, burning through the clouds on fire. A moment before it had been blue and calm, but suddenly the entire sky was exploding, as far as I could see, reaching from the jungle all the way across the ocean.

The light was nearly blinding as the yellow and orange flames licked overhead, burning through the atmosphere. I heard Fang inhale sharply next to me, and we both stared in awe and wonder. Seconds felt like hours as we watched the whole horizon transform into a raging inferno.

I could not move.

It was...dazzling. More than that. It was awesomely, terrifyingly beautiful. Like, it hurt to look at. The most spectacular sunset the world would ever see—this was the world's final good night.

Moments later, a gash ripped across the sky, splitting it into two flaming halves, with an aching hole of nothingness between them. Then the split opened wider, like a horrible, garish sneer, and I felt all the dread I'd been bottling up sigh right out of it. I held my breath as I waited for the hand of God, or aliens, or even vindictive Ari, back from the dead one last time, to reach out and pluck me from where I stood.

Instead, from that gaping mouth came a wave of excruciating heat that swept through the jungle and right over us.

I snapped out of my trance and collapsed to the floor in agony, tearing at my feathers, my clothes; I was sure my skin was boiling off. I couldn't even scream—my lungs were like shriveled little steaks baking inside my chest.

I was hyperventilating, trying desperately to breathe. Everything was getting fuzzy, except the pain. I was passing out.

But after what felt like a century of torture, the gap zipped closed as quickly as it had opened.

I gagged, sucking in the cooling air. I was alive. With intact skin and feathers. How was that even possible? I squinted upward, disbelieving. Except for some dying red streaks, the fire was no longer scorching the sky.

My adrenaline finally caught up to the insanity and the world rushed back into place. I scrambled to my feet, looking around wildly. I didn't know what I was looking for—just an answer, a direction I could follow.

"Everybody's at the caves!" Fang wheezed over the now furious wind. Smoke and ash billowed around us.

I shook my head stubbornly. "Not Angel," I croaked, my throat raw. Fang looked me in the eye and saw what else I couldn't say: *Or Dylan.*

They'd be at the cliffs, rounding up the rest of the community.

Like I should've been from the start.

Together, in silent agreement, Fang and I shot into the sky. A few hundred meters away, all the trees were scorched—a few more seconds of that heat and we would've been human fireworks. As we raced over the smoking jungle toward the coastline, we saw trees crashed down on one another like dominoes. Their trunks were stripped of bark and branches from where the fire had come.

Suddenly then there was a bang like nothing I'd ever heard—like a bomb connected to an amp had been detonated right inside my skull. It sounded like what the fiery explosion should've sounded like, but it came more than a full minute later.

It was like I'd been shot.

I felt it in my teeth, and vibrating through my brain.

I felt it in my wings as I flapped and spun uncontrollably.

It sang through my eardrums and made my eyes blur.

And then we were falling.

Down.

Down.

Like Angel knew we would.

I watched, helpless, as the ash whirled around and the jutting precipice of rock raced up to meet me.

Then the eyes of the world winked shut.

85

GET UP, A fuzzy voice shrieked. *Get up get up get up.* It sounded water-soaked, low and slow. Was it my Voice, or Angel's, or someone else's entirely? I didn't even know if it was real

The ringing in my head grew, turning into a sound like the hiss of rushing water, an echo bouncing around like a rubber ball inside my head. Wind whipped around me and the hiss grew to a wail. My brain throbbed.

I covered my ears and felt wetness. The metallic smell of blood burned in my nostrils. I pried open my eyes, and that's when the hurricane-strength needles of rain started to hit my face.

I turned to look for help and felt my stomach lurch as a strong arm yanked me back, keeping me from plummeting over the edge of the cliff. "Get up!" Fang yelled in my face, finally piercing through my confusion and dragging me to my feet.

I looked across the cliffs for the other kids, but saw only a wall of water out in the sea. Not just a wall—a massive wall, miles long and taller than a skyscraper. Surrounding us. The monstrous wave grew more massive by the second, almost blotting out the smoking sky as it surged toward the precarious crag we clung to.

A mega-tsunami.

I instinctively tried to flap, but a searing pain shot through my mangled, bleeding wing. Panic froze my heart. This was it.

There would be no more.

I felt a sob of self-pity building in my chest, but Fang held my face in his hands and looked at me urgently, his eyes locked on mine.

"I love you, Max," Fang said, and those words, the ones I'd been waiting to hear forever, towered above all the chaos, making everything else fall away. Whole universes were built and destroyed by those words. There were tears in his eyes. "God, Max, I love you so much."

I know, I thought. *I've always known.*

Then Fang's stormy eyes grew blacker than I'd ever seen them as they looked past me, at our fate. I turned to see the wave swelling toward us, seconds away, the white foam of its mouth howling higher and higher. But I wasn't surprised, or scared, or even angry. I accepted it like a friendly wind, come to fly me home.

It's okay, I thought. And it was.

Fang kissed my eyelids, my cheeks, and then my lips one more time, whisper soft. Then he clutched my head to his chest and we took one last deep breath, wrapping ourselves in each other's arms for eternity as the warm water crashed over the cliff and swallowed us whole.

I love you, too, Fang.

Epilogue
MAX'S
LAST
WORDS

NOW, DON'T GET all weepy on me, dear reader. No chin-quivering or nose-sniveling, either. These pages do not need to be all soggy with your mucus.

There's nothing to moan and groan about, anyway. The truth is, I am the luckiest girl in the world.

Don't give me that I-can-see-right-through-you-Max-and-not-just-because-you're-freaking-dead look. I'm serious.

Think about it. When the end comes, will you be buried in the arms of the one you love? Of the one who knew you your whole life, who loved you your whole life? The one person who could really and truly love you like you needed to be loved?

I hope so.

Because I was, and I wouldn't change any of it—not for anything.

Not even the world.

Okay, I can see that you're upset. I know you must be wondering, just like I'm wondering right now: Was I really supposed to save the world, or was it all just a big lie?

In other words, did I fail? (Gosh, it sounds so ugly when you put it like that.)

Or was my life just a metaphor for what we're *all* supposed to do with our lives—that each of us is supposed to believe that we *can*, that we *must* save the world? That the world will be saved only if we *each* take that kind of responsibility?

Because if this life has taught me anything, it's that we can't leave anything up to fate or chance, or for someone else to clean up. Because in the end, "special" people are still just people. Because, PS, those so-called special people *can't* actually save us.

We all have to save ourselves.

Or maybe this was a lesson in carpe ever-loving diem—*seize the day*, kiddos, and hold tight to your loved ones, the only part of life that really matters, and live each moment to the fullest, because you never know when an explosive ball of gas is going to light up the sky and blow you into oblivion.

But no, really.

Was it all just a big shrug of meaninglessness that will now plunge you into a pit of existential emptiness and melancholy?

I hope not. At least, don't blame me for it. What, carrying the weight of the whole world wasn't enough? I have to look out for your happiness, too?

Jokes aside, I really do hope that my life meant something in the end—that it meant *all* of those things. I don't know what's next—what any of us can expect—but I do know that I'm ready to see what's out there for me. In fact, I think I hear Fang calling my name now. He sounds so far away....

You guys? I don't want to, like, freak you out at this point in our journey, but I think I'm starting to see that famous light at the end of the tunnel that you always hear about. This is where we part ways, I'm afraid.

Before I go, even if you've rolled your eyes at every bit of cheesy advice I pulled out of my butt when the flock needed some pep in their patooties these last few years, know that I mean this last little nugget from the bottom of my not-really-so-cynical little freak heart:

Save your world. Love it, protect it, and respect it, and don't let haters represent it.

Don't leave the saving to anyone else, ever, because, exhibit A—why, hello there!—*it's way too much for one person.* And if you want to skip out on the responsibility train, my whole life—and death—will have been in vain.

It's yours. It's all yours for the taking!

You're not going to waste it now, are you?

Epilogue the Last

THE
BEGINNING

One

WHEN I OPEN my eyes, everything is dim blue wonder. Playful shapes of light dance across my vision, diving, and dipping, then merging into shadow. I thought heaven would be brighter.

I'm spinning, and I watch in bug-eyed wonder as my hand moves in front of my face in slow motion, my fingers leaving streaks like sparkler trails in the dark as my eyes try to adjust to their movement.

I can feel the air as I push and poke, think I can taste the sound of what blue feels like—a whale's warbling echo.

Or is that singing?

Of course *my* angels sound like strangled whales.

It's wonderful feeling weightless, free. Almost like flying, but without even having to move—floating toward an easy, carefree eternity of being rocked like a baby, free of all burdens and responsibility. I actually sigh with relief.

Wait a minute. I just *sighed*. I'm...breathing?

Underwater?

I'm alive?

"Max," I hear a voice call from above. What a magical sound that is.

Hmm? I think. *Voice, is that you pestering me again? Do not disturb. Busy floating. Call if you want to talk rainbows.*

A disembodied hand grasps mine and pulls me upward.

Are you there, God? It's me, Max.

"Max!" The voice is clearer, immediate.

The water cradles me closer. *Am I moving at all? Is this real?*

My eyes trace slowly, lazily up the hand that's entwined with mine, the squared fingers tan and vaguely familiar. And strong. Like the arm and shoulder the hand is connected to. The face finally registers just as we break the surface.

As does shock.

Thrashing, I stupidly suck in a huge breath through my nose, instead of using the gills I developed long ago. The harsh air rips through my lungs, and I double over, coughing and choking out water.

"I told you I would come back for you," Dylan whispers, rubbing my back.

Two

FANG, DYLAN, ANGEL, and I sit perched on a large, exposed ridge of rock that rises high out of the water. We're alive. A little soggy and a lot banged up, maybe, but still living, breathing.

Survivors.

Hawks soar above us, diving through the narrow crevices, their long brown feathers mirroring my own. As the sun warms my face, I long to join them.

I peer out over the vast strangeness of the landscape, a charred wasteland: the island, now broken up into hundreds of smaller islands, with narrow inlets snaking in and out of them; the spindly remaining trees, branchless, barkless, standing straight up like frightened soldiers with an army of dead brothers at their feet; the hardening ash, swirling into surreal silver spirals, hot air belching out of cracks in the crust to form thermal pools; and an unfathomable high-tech city of luxury, sealed in caves that are now buried below the turquoise water.

It's been only a few hours since the Split—when the gash in the sky severed this new world from the old one—but we swam and limped and swerved into our new existence feeling changed.

But we haven't changed, really; the rest of the world has. And somehow, this new world makes sense in a way that the old one never did.

Fang's tying a singed but sturdy branch to my wing with a scrap of his T-shirt, creating a splint. My wing, though still painful, is already healing before my eyes. Because it was *made* to. We are not fragile creatures, after all.

And that is why we're still here.

Dylan is watching Fang's movements—deft, efficient—but there's no threat there. Something has shifted.

In all of us.

"I read about something like this happening in Russia," Dylan says, answering the question we're all asking in our heads: What, exactly, was that *thing* that split our world in two? "The Tunguska event, I think it was, in the early twentieth century. A meteor exploded near the earth's surface and wiped out miles and miles of forest."

I can't help but notice how confident he sounds, how he doesn't look down when he talks, how he's no longer embarrassed about his interest in science, his love of books. He's just eager to share the knowledge that will help the group survive. He knows, as we all do, that we can use any help we can get.

"This seems a lot bigger than that one, though," he says. "I wonder if anything like this is happening elsewhere— like a ripple effect or something. Just look at the sky. I've definitely never read about anything like that."

The sky has taken on this bizarre, Technicolor hue that warps and shimmers like some psychedelic black-light poster—totally surreal. Yet…it feels familiar, somehow. Like I've been dreaming about it every night of my life, but I've just forgotten my dreams each day on waking to the life in which I have been trapped.

I keep thinking how amazing this place is going to be to explore by air.

Dylan stands up. "We should probably start combing the perimeter for possible other entrances to the caves. The main line I took everybody through is now underwater."

"I'll check out the tree-house village," Fang says. "See if there's anything left, start the rebuilding." He gives my hand a tight squeeze, but that desperation, that urgency between us is gone. No insecurities. Max and Fang. Fang and Max. No longer a question. We just *are*.

Angel and I sit together on the edge, watching the guys soar through the air. We don't need to talk, because every-thing is understood. The weirdness that had come between us is gone, and since resurfacing I haven't heard a word from my Voice, trying to tell me what to do. There's no leader now, no power. We're all working—quickly, efficiently—together.

It's well documented that I've never been very good at school or any of the other junk normal kids are supposed to slog through. That's because I'm *not* normal, and never have been. None of us are. But in this postapocalyptic world, on this tiny, wrecked island, I have a feeling we're going to excel.

"Dylan's right that this thing's big," Angel says after a few minutes. "I'm tapping into Dr. Martinez's thoughts, and they're monitoring satellite connections all over the world from inside the caves. This wasn't the only event. It's triggered a ripple effect. There's been major volcanic and tectonic activity. Whole countries may be covered in water, ash, or flame. It's unclear at this point."

The two of us are silent for a long moment, letting that sink in—that the whole world and probably most of the people we know in it are done for.

"I'm so glad that it wasn't me, that it wasn't us," Angel says, her eyes brimming with tears. "Isn't that selfish?"

I shake my head. "It's not selfish. *We're* here. *We're* alive. I'm not going to apologize for surviving." That might sound harsh, but through the grief and the devastation, I can't help feeling hope, too. If you could choose between life and death, wouldn't you leap toward living with everything you had?

No one wanted life as we knew it to end. But we were

made for this. Surviving, I mean. And the truth is, we weren't that great at fitting in to life as we knew it, anyway. In fact, life as we knew it kind of sucked. Stuck in cages, trackers implanted beneath our skin, all that power they shoveled between us, turning us into sideshow freaks.

That's all over now. The whitecoats only know how to live in a world where they can have cushy homes and order factory-farmed, premade food. This is definitely not their world.

It's ours.

"I know what you mean," Angel says, reading my thoughts. Her blue eyes have a faraway look, and even without the ash in her feathers, she looks older, more mature. Like she grew a century in an hour. Like she grew into that Voice of hers. "It's almost like we were meant for this world, and not that other one. Like it's finally our time."

It's a dark thought, but one I can't turn away from. This is an environment that requires a little something extra from its inhabitants. Half of it is underwater. And we have *gills*. The other half is made of unreachable cliffs and towering trees. And we have *wings*. This place is primal, and it's raw.

I was made for this.

And if I'm going to start this new life being who I am truly meant to be, there is something I know I have to do.

I look beyond Angel's windblown curls and see that Fang has returned and is looking at me.

I walk over to him, our gazes fully locked. And when I

reach him, I don't hesitate to say what I know is the most important truth of my life. The only truth.

"I love you, Fang," I whisper.

He smiles and takes my hand.

We stand together on the precipice, opening our wings to their full span and watching the long feathery shadows reach out over the land below.

In a way, maybe I did die in that wet grave, because it's like I was completely reborn when I came up from that water. The air feels different to me now. I'm breathing it differently now. Like my body is a whole new machine.

It *is* my time.

The time of Maximum Ride.

SHE SAYS SHE'S INNOCENT.

THE POLICE DON'T BELIEVE HER.

HER OWN BROTHERS DON'T BELIEVE HER.

YOU PROBABLY WON'T, EITHER.